“How long d

“I don’t know.” He

takes.”

All he wanted was to get back to Houston where his parents needed him. He didn’t have time to camp out in Medina and appease the twins’ aunt. But they obviously didn’t trust each other and how else could they ever work this out, living four hours apart?

“Here’s an idea. I could work for you, building furniture or as a ranch hand. While I work for you, I could get to know my niece and nephew. How does that sound?”

“Too good to be true.” Her eyes narrowed. “Do you have a criminal record?”

He laughed. “I’m the older, wiser brother. I spent the first twenty years of my life cleaning up Ron’s messes. I guess I still am in a way.”

“My niece and nephew are not messes.”

“That’s not what I meant. The situation is a mess. That he never told me or my folks they existed.”

Something in her eyes softened. “If you’re serious about the job…you’re hired.”

Shannon Taylor Vannatter is a stay-at-home mom, pastor's wife and award-winning author. She lives in a rural central Arkansas community with a population of around one hundred, if you count a few cows. Contact her at shannonvannatter.com.

Books by Shannon Taylor Vannatter

Love Inspired

Hill Country Cowboys

Hill Country Redemption
The Cowboy's Missing Memory
A Texas Bond

Texas Cowboys

Reuniting with the Cowboy
Winning Over the Cowboy
A Texas Holiday Reunion
Counting on the Cowboy

Love Inspired Heartsong Presents

Rodeo Ashes
Rodeo Regrets
Rodeo Queen
Rodeo Song
Rodeo Family
Rodeo Reunion

Visit the Author Profile page at Harlequin.com.

A Texas Bond

Shannon Taylor Vannatter

LOVE INSPIRED®
INSPIRATIONAL ROMANCE

Recycling programs for this product may not exist in your area.

ISBN-13: 978-1-335-48876-3

A Texas Bond

This edition published by arrangement with Harlequin Books S.A.

For questions and comments about the quality of this book, please contact us at CustomerService@Harlequin.com.

Love Inspired
22 Adelaide St. West, 40th Floor
Toronto, Ontario M5H 4E3, Canada
www.Harlequin.com

Printed in U.S.A.

Train up a child in the way he should go:
and when he is old, he will not depart from it.

—*Proverbs* 22:6

I dedicate this book to readers.
Without y'all, I wouldn't get to do this.

Chapter One

"Great bones." The upholstery tacks popped loose with a satisfying thwack, releasing dust in a cloud around Stacia Keyes's head. She readjusted her mask as she pulled the ancient fabric and batting away from the wingback chair.

"What a beauty." Daddy looked up from the bookshelf he was building out of old chippy-painted window shutters. "She'll soon be regal again."

"What do you think of this fabric?" Stacia laid the rose gold-and-taupe-striped upholstery over the back.

"Freshen the legs with mahogany stain, and she'll be a perfect addition to 3 Gals' Treasures." Daddy used the nail gun to secure a bead board panel to the shutters.

Her mom's dream antique and vintage shop—now Stacia's since her mom and her sister were both gone—was in the heart of Medina, Texas Hill Country. Along with Daddy's demolition business, the store specialized in repurposing salvaged materials.

"We have an update on heavy metal rock star, Ronny Outrageous."

Her attention zeroed in on the TV as the breath stilled in her lungs. A picture of him in full goth makeup popped up beside the blond news anchor. Daddy grabbed the remote, bumped up the sound.

"As we reported, last weekend Ronny Outrageous was in a deadly tour bus accident. His condition has continued to stabilize and the fan favorite was moved from the ICU into a private room today. Fans have flooded city parks across Los Angeles and his home state of Texas. holding vigil for the heavy metal singer."

A shot of the accident site piled with cards, flowers and stuffed animals filled the screen followed by a clip of a crowd of well-wishers holding smartphones, swaying in unison.

"As #GetWellRonny trends across social media, fans hold placards of love and affection, waiting, hoping to be interviewed so the singer can hear their sentiments."

The television went dark.

"That's enough of that." Daddy set the remote down.

"What if he comes for the twins?" Her greatest fear since he'd signed them over to her after her sister died three years ago.

"Don't go borrowing trouble." Daddy gave her hand a squeeze. "He signed away his rights. Twice. They're five now. Since he hasn't wanted them all these years, he's not going to start now."

"Facing death changes people." Her voice cracked.

"Some folks are too selfish to change. He'll recover and get on with his career." Daddy went back to work on the bookshelf. The thwack of his nail gun filled the air for the next several minutes, and then he picked up the level, checking each side. "I forgot to tell you I saw Adrian at the grocery store the other day. He asked about you. Always does."

"I don't know why. He's the one who broke things off."

"It's perfectly normal for a single guy to get nervous

when the girl he's dating takes on twins to raise. But things have settled down now. Maybe you could give him another chance."

"He told me he wanted his own kids to raise, not someone else's, Daddy. That's pretty straightforward." She hadn't been serious about Adrian and never told him she'd inherited her mom's heart defect. "I told you I was about to break things off anyway. We weren't a good match."

"You have no idea how proud I am of you for taking on the responsibility of raising Mason and Madison. I mean, at the tender age of twenty-five you took on not one, but twin two-year-olds and they've thrived in the past three years."

"They're my niece and nephew. Anyone would have done the same."

"Maybe." Daddy tested the stability and joints of the shelf. "But I want you to live a full life. To have a love like I had with your mother. God has someone for you, who will love you and the twins and be content without biological children. You just need to open your heart to the possibility."

"I'm fine the way things are. I have the twins and you. That's all I need." But a pang settled in her heart the way it always did when she thought of never having cousins for the twins.

As a Christian, it wasn't that she was afraid to die, but she refused to take the chance of leaving motherless children behind. Enough of that had happened in her family already.

"But I won't be around forever and the kids will grow up and be gone some day."

"Now you're depressing me." She ripped the final piece of upholstery off the back of the chair.

"I just don't want you to miss out on your own happily-ever-after." He touched her arm. "Don't get me wrong, I wouldn't take anything for you and the years we had with your sister. But I loved your mother and if we'd known back then about her heart condition, I'd have married her anyway and been willing to adopt."

But Daddy was one of a kind. A man who'd raised two daughters alone, despite a manipulative sister-in-law. He could have handed them over to Aunt Eleanor and waltzed off into the sunset. A lot of men would have.

It was easier just to avoid men, not risk her heart, emotionally or physically.

"Just think about it."

She nodded to appease him. But the most pressing thing on her mind was Ron having a change of heart about the twins. Her stomach clenched.

"That's my girl." He checked his watch. "Time to open."

"I'll be there as soon as I clean up." She slipped her smock off. Thankfully, her capris and blouse were none the worse for wear. In the bathroom, she dabbed a wet washcloth over her face, attempting not to wash off her makeup, then soaped the grime from her arms and hands.

Leaving the back door of the workshop open for ventilation, she entered the front part of the barn that housed the store. Long aisles were packed with everything from a flat-bottom boat repurposed into a bookshelf to an old upright piano turned into a desk to various antiques and vintage furnishings.

Daddy perched on the stool behind the counter.

Every clock in the place chimed ten times as she hurried to unlock the front door and turn the Open sign around.

Waverly Heathcott stood outside, waiting. One of their

best and possibly richest customers, owner of The Texas Rose. Definitely the most put together.

While Stacia sported mottled skin with blotchy cheeks. A testament that Texas hadn't caught on that it was almost mid-September and she was a natural redhead and didn't perspire much. Her hair spilled from a messy bun with damp tendrils around her face. She blew a long layer out of her eyes. Oh well, she looked like she worked hard. Not everyone could be runway ready all the time like Waverly.

"Come in." Stacia opened the door for her. "Sorry, we were in the workshop or I'd have let you in already."

"No worries. I'm early. I was wondering how many—" Waverly stopped in front of a coffee bar constructed from an old door, a small table, spindles and corbels. "Oh, Stasha, I'm in love with this." She tucked a strand of perfect blond hair behind her ear. "How many of them do you have?"

"Just the one at the moment." No matter how many times Stacia reminded her it was pronounced Stay-shuh, Waverly continued to say her name as if it rhymed with Tasha.

"They fly out the door as soon as I build them." Daddy scratched his graying beard.

"I'm remodeling The Texas Rose." Waverly continued on to the counter.

"Which one?" Stacia asked. Waverly had been a frequent shopper over the years as she'd opened each of her twenty shabby chic–style bed-and-breakfasts scattered across Texas.

"All of them. Could I get one of those for each room?"

Stacia squelched a gasp. "That's one hundred rooms. Right?"

"Yes."

"I'm afraid we can't build them exactly the same."

"Of course not. If I wanted carbon copies, I wouldn't be here." Waverly glanced around the store. "That's what I love about this place, everything is unique."

"Still shabby chic, right?"

"Definitely."

Stacia grabbed her tablet from under the counter and pulled up an order form. "Ninety-nine shabby chic coffee bars."

"In white with pink, blush, seafoam, lavender and yellow trim. I brought fabric swatches." Waverly handed them to her.

"Great. Let's go to my workshop to pick paint tabs and I need you to browse the warehouse with me, so I can get a feel for the types of materials you like."

"My favorite part." Waverly followed, glamorous in her white pants suit and spiked heels.

The bell rang and a man stepped inside. A handsome man. Close to Stacia's age.

"May I help you?" Daddy hurried over.

Stacia ushered Waverly into the workshop. Half-finished repurposed projects dotted the space in the back of the barn, everything from a bistro table and chairs to a vintage sofa and a pile of claw-foot tubs needing resurfacing. The stuffy stillness made her regret leaving the door open. She shut it and turned the air conditioner on. The cool blast swept chill bumps over her.

"Sorry about the temperature. Even with the ventilation system, it gets so dusty in here, so I was trying to air it out."

"It's fine."

Not just any customer was allowed in the workshop. But it wasn't the first time Waverly Heathcott had strolled through it and the warehouse full of rusty metal gates, finials, vintage doors, windows and shutters. Though it had never happened, Stacia always worried she'd get a dry cleaning bill.

"Oh, I almost forgot what I came for. I also need one hundred claw-foot tubs. Is that all you have?" She pointed at the pile.

"There are five in the store already finished, plus these for a total of twenty-three."

"Can you get more?"

"I'm certain we can. I'll put a call out to vendors I know, but it may take time."

"Is a month enough time?"

Stacia swallowed hard. "A month?"

"That's my timeline for the remodel. I'll be shut down for six weeks and I want everything in place before we reopen."

"You want ninety-nine coffee bars and ninety-five restored claw-foot bathtubs in a month?" Stacia tried to calculate a schedule in her head.

"I know it's a lot, but if anyone can pull it off, 3 Gals' Treasures can." Waverly flashed her best I'm-rich-just-make-it-happen smile.

"You came to the right place."

Over the next thirty minutes, they picked paint and Waverly chose pieces and parts she liked for the coffee bars as Stacia snapped pictures and added details to the order. They agreed on a price and Waverly paid half down.

How to tell Daddy? Not only were they short-staffed, but she'd just agreed to an impossible order.

She led Waverly back to the store.

"Thank you, you're a treasure." Waverly gave her a quick hug. "I can't wait to see what you create."

"We'll ship the bathtubs we have, and more as we complete them, so you'll have time for installation. As we complete the coffee bars, I'll send pictures for your approval."

"I'll love whatever you come up with. I always do." With a wave, Waverly strolled to the exit.

As Stacia headed to the register, she saw the man. Still there. And completely focused on her twin niece and nephew who were now sitting behind the counter. Something felt familiar about his dark hair and features, paired with emerald eyes. A chill went down the back of her neck.

"There she is. She'll be right with you," Daddy said.

"Aunt Stacia!" the twins shouted in unison and rushed her.

"When did y'all get here?" She knelt to hug them.

"Aunt Larae dropped us off. She didn't want us to get sick cuz Jayda started sneezing this morning," Madison reported. "She said it's probably allergies, but just in case, she brought us home."

"Do y'all feel okay?" She pressed a palm to each of their foreheads. Both cool.

"Yep," their voices blended.

Saturdays were a real challenge since her clerk had married her ranch hand and moved to Waco. Now that they were shorthanded, the twins often spent Friday night and the following day at her friend's ranch. But sometimes that didn't work out. Like today, making Stacia wish she and Daddy could leave the store in someone else's hands and spend the day with them.

But weekends were always busy. The usual rush before and after lunch required two clerks in the showroom while Daddy helped customers load purchases.

"If you'll be real good—that means no running, giggling or squealing—I'll get Grandpa to take y'all to get ice cream."

"Ice cream!" Mason jumped up and down. "Before lunch?"

"Just this once, we'll have a late lunch." She winked. "But that includes no jumping."

Mason quickly stilled.

"We'll be extra good," Madison promised. "Won't we, Mason?"

Mason nodded. Always the weak link. It wasn't that he was bad. Just mischievous, full of energy and easily bored. Which usually got him in trouble. A lot like his mom had been.

She ushered the children ahead of her and they dutifully returned to their seats behind the counter.

Daddy hurried toward her, lowering his voice to a whisper. "He wants to talk to you. Hasn't browsed or anything, just patiently waited for you. Maybe he's here about a job. An answer to our prayers."

"I hope so. Waverly wants the coffee bar and all five of the claw-foot tubs we have finished. Plus she ordered ninety-nine more bars and ninety-five more tubs."

"That's awesome."

"She wants all of it in a month."

"Tell me you didn't agree to those terms."

Stacia winced. "I've got a nice check in my pocket."

"Aye yai yai. You better hope he's here for a job."

The man waited at the counter, his gaze still riveted on the twins. Nothing new there. Both strawberry blond, freckled, large blue-green eyes, obviously twins—carbon copies of one another except for gender. Double the cuteness factor.

"I'm Stacia Keyes." She offered her hand.

He tore his attention away from the children. "Ross Lyles. Nice to meet you."

The last name sent a jolt through her heart. No. Ron didn't have any family.

Intense green eyes scrutinized her as his hand engulfed hers in a firm grip.

"Are you interested in the ranch hand position? Or the furniture handyman position?"

"Huh?" His gaze darted back to the kids.

"Do you have experience in either?"

"Actually both." He cleared his throat.

Daddy chuckled. "You're hired."

"Daddy." This guy was way too focused on her niece and nephew. "We usually get references on new hires."

"I know, but we're in a real pickle. Can't afford to be too choosy."

"Why don't you take the kids to get ice cream? I told them you would if they were good in the store." Both had been quiet as a mouse, staring back at Ross Lyles. She wanted them out of his sight. And rid of Daddy's big mouth.

"Sounds like a plan, once Angel gets here."

"Shouldn't she be here by now?" Stacia checked her watch.

"She called, said her car's still in the shop and her mom had to go in to work early, so she's driving their farm truck and it didn't want to start this morning."

A pickup badly in need of a new muffler sounded out front. "Sounds like she just pulled up."

"I scream, you scream, we all scream for ice cream." Daddy waggled his eyebrows at the twins, eliciting a fit of giggles.

"Shh." Madison caught herself, tried to shush Mason. "No giggles in the store or we don't get ice cream."

"I don't think that rule counts when I'm the one who made you giggle." Daddy came out from behind the counter. "Let's go. What flavor do y'all want?"

"I want cotton candy." Mason darted for the door.

"No running," Madison cautioned. "I want bubble gum."

"It was nice to meet you, Ross."

"Likewise, Maverick."

He was already on a first-name basis with her dad?

The door closed behind them. And only then did Ross Lyles's gaze return to hers.

Was he somehow related to Ron? Here on a spy mission for him? Or was Lyles even really his last name? He could be some random nut who'd gotten wind of a scandal. An obsessed fan, reporter or blackmailer. Foreboding crept up the back of her neck. She squelched a shudder. There's no way she could hire him.

"I'm afraid I already hired someone for both positions this morning. My dad didn't know, so I'm sorry if he got your hopes up."

He did a slight shake of his head. As if to wake himself up from a trance. "I'm—"

Nothing else came out of his mouth. This guy was creeping her out. And there were no other customers in the store. Angel, the eighty-pound teenager, wouldn't be any help, if she ever made it inside. Stacia needed to get rid of him. Fast.

Ross tried to focus. It was tempting to pretend he was here for the jobs. Since he'd worked at his grandfather's ranch and his parents' furniture store, he was qualified for both. And he had an inkling both positions were still open. If not, surely she'd have told her dad. Or at least taken the sign out of the window. And she wouldn't have asked him about experience. But he'd already gotten her suspicious. Did she know who he was?

No. Ron hadn't used his real name in years. Except maybe on legal documents. Like when he signed the twins away. They looked similar, but Ron wore thick black eyeliner and kept his dark hair dyed blue, which would throw anybody off.

So tempting to play his name off as a coincidence. Talk her into hiring him. That way, he'd have a direct window into her interactions with the twins.

"Can I help you with anything else?"

Best to come clean. "Are you familiar with the name Ronny Outrageous?"

She caved in on herself, as if someone had kicked her in the stomach. "Why?"

"Because he's my brother."

"Oh." Something akin to fear shone in her pale aqua eyes.

"Last week, he was in a really bad bus wreck with an eighteen-wheeler on the way to a concert."

"I heard about it on the news." She tried to recover, act all calm, cool and collected. But it was too late. Her reaction to Ron's stage name told the tale.

"One long, dark, pain-filled night he made a confession to me. That he'd had a one-night stand, which resulted in twins." The more information he gave, the more certain he was that he'd found the right Stacia Keyes.

"That he signed custody over to the mother. That she died three years ago." The children's pale coloring had thrown him off since his family had olive skin and dark hair. "That her sister has them now. Sounding familiar?"

"What do you want?" She sank into a chair behind the counter, as if her legs would no longer hold her up, pushed damp, auburn tendrils away from her face.

"For now, I just want to get to know my niece and nephew." To make sure they're well taken care of. And if not, he'd fight for them.

She'd turned positively green and he felt kind of sorry

for her. Whether she took good care of the children or not, she definitely loved them.

A bell rang at the front of the store and a teenage girl stepped inside. “Sorry, I’m late. That truck hates me.” Her gaze pinged back and forth between him and Stacia. “Is everything okay?”

“Fine. Daddy took the kids for ice cream. Could you watch the store for a bit, Angel?”

“Sure.”

“We’ll just be in the workshop.” She stood, motioned for him to follow.

At the back of the barn, they exited into a dusty space filled with tools, a worktable, project pieces. He couldn’t tell if they were in the middle of being put together or torn apart.

“He said he didn’t have any family.” She sank into a wooden chair, covered her face with both hands.

“We’ve been estranged for several years.” Since their parents had tried to get Ron in rehab, he’d wanted nothing to do with any of his family. So to him, he probably felt like a loner. He’d patched things up with them after his accident. Only because he needed someone to take care of him once he got out of the hospital. For the moment, he was clean. At least until he could get back out on the road.

Her hands dropped into her lap. “Does he want them back?”

“No. He wishes he hadn’t told me.”

She blew out a big breath, obviously relieved.

More than anything, he didn’t want to intimidate her. “But let me assure you, my folks would be very interested in the children.” He found a chair that matched hers, pulled it over and sat, so she wouldn’t feel as if he were talking down to her. “If they knew about them, that is.”

“They don’t know?”

"I thought I'd come check things out before I involve them."

"Daddy and I have been a major part of their lives since they were born." Fear took root in her expressive eyes. "They're happy with us."

"That's what I'm here to find out."

"And then what?" Her voice quivered.

"I don't know yet." It all depended on if the twins were well cared for. "What do they know about Ron?"

"Nothing much." She stood, paced the trail between projects. "They asked once about a year ago. Daddy told them their father has a really important, time-consuming job."

"I guess that's better than saying he's a self-centered jerk."

"How long do you plan to stay?"

"I don't know that either." He shrugged. "However long it takes."

"Don't you have a job or someone to get back to?"

"I'm a furniture builder and designer at my parents' furniture store in Houston. I told them I needed some time off." They actually thought he was at his grandfather's in Hondo helping out at his ranch. And with the store in high demand, the timing had been terrible. He'd seen it in their eyes; they thought he wanted to leave the business. Just like Ron.

As for someone, not anymore. Nora had accused him of seeing someone else for the last time. After her, he might not date ever again. Especially not anyone jealous, distrustful or insecure.

Staying definitely wasn't on his schedule. He had to get back to Houston where his parents needed him, and he was eager to prove their fears wrong. He didn't have time to camp out in Medina and appease the twins' aunt that he was an okay guy. But they obviously didn't trust each other and how else could they ever work this out living four hours apart?

"Here's an idea. I could work for you, building furniture or as a ranch hand or both since I have experience in both areas. While I work for you, I could get to know my niece and nephew. How does that sound?"

"Too good to be true. I mean—the part where you have experience in both positions I need to fill." Her eyes narrowed. "For all I know, you could be a reporter sniffing out a story or a blackmailer for that matter."

He slipped his phone out of his pocket, scrolled through it, then showed her a picture of him with Ron in the hospital. "Our mom took that. It had been several years since we'd been together for a photo op." Ron's typical makeup made him look even paler than normal.

"That doesn't mean anything. You could be an obsessed fan who snuck into the hospital for all I know."

"An obsessed fan who happens to have the same last name as Ronny Outrageous aka Ron Lyles?" He showed her his driver's license. "And trust me, there's no sneaking into that hospital." Ron's manager had hired security, but so far fans hadn't figured out where Ron was. "Besides, if I were a blackmailer, I'd be talking to Ron. He's the one with money and a potential scandal to hide." He scrolled on his phone again. "Here, read the text with the photo."

Here's the pic I took of my two boys in the hospital. Does a mother's heart good to have the two of you together again.

"Okay, looks like you're who you say you are. But do you have a criminal record?"

"Good one." He tilted his head back with a belly laugh.

"I'm the older, wiser brother. I spent the first twenty years of my life cleaning up Ron's messes. I guess I still am in a way."

"My niece and nephew are not messes you need to clean up." Her gaze hardened. "They're children. And they're perfectly happy without you."

"That's not what I meant. The situation is a mess. That he signed them away—twice." He let out a heavy sigh. "And never told me or my folks they existed. Until a weak moment when he thought he was dying."

Something in her eyes softened. "Just give me a chance to explain things to my dad. And if you're serious about the job, you're hired."

"I am, but what about your new hires?"

Pink tinged her cheeks. "I made that up. You were freaking me out staring at the twins."

At least she was protective. "What time do you open?"

"Ten and we stay open until six. Every day but Sunday. One or both of us are usually in the workshop by seven or eight."

"I'll be here. But instead of leaving and coming back tonight, what if I stick around tonight while you tell them?"

"I'm not comfortable with that." She hugged herself.

"Well maybe I'm not comfortable leaving it to you. You might tell them I'm some ogre who's come to take them away. Or smuggle them out of town and move somewhere else to keep me away."

She got that deer caught in the headlights look for a moment. "I haven't known you long enough to know if you're an ogre or not and I'd be lying if I said running hasn't crossed my mind in the last five minutes. But only for a moment. This is their home and I'd never uproot them for a life of hiding, with legal consequences if we were caught." She grabbed the broom, swept the dusty floor.

"If I was an ogre, I wouldn't be here. I'd have contacted a lawyer and taken you straight to court for a custody battle. But I didn't." To be honest, if they were still babies, he probably would have. But the twins were five. "Their lives have always been here with you and your father as the two constants. I don't want to disrupt that. Unless I find they're not being well cared for or are abused."

"I can assure you that's not the case," she hissed.

"All I want is to be part of their lives. I really think we can work through this very difficult situation together and do what's best for my niece and nephew. And the first step to that is to tell them who I am."

She closed her eyes, leaned on her broom. "Come to the house around seven tonight. That'll give me time to talk to Daddy and you can have supper with us."

"The farmhouse next door?"

"Yes."

"I'll be there. But supper isn't necessary. I don't want to intrude."

"You've already done that." Her stiff posture was in full Mama Bear mode.

"This isn't easy for me either, you know?"

"No, I guess it's not." She swept the pile of debris into a dust pan, dumped it in the trash. "Where are you staying?"

"I'm renting a nightly cabin in Bandera at the moment, but if I stick around very long, I'll find something else more long-term."

"I'll see you at seven." Her eyes said she hoped he'd move on. But he couldn't. His niece and nephew deserved to know about him. About his parents. The twins had seemed fine in the store earlier, but he couldn't be at peace until he knew for certain they were happy, healthy and loved. Somehow, he had to work this out with complete strangers.

Chapter Two

"How do we tell them about this new uncle showing up, without getting into the subject of their father?" Daddy settled heavily on the couch in the great room, covered his face with his hands.

"I'm not sure, but he'll be here soon, so we need to figure it out." Stacia, on autopilot, set the casserole dish in the center of the table in the adjoining kitchen.

"Are you sure he's telling the truth? That he's not some reporter?"

She filled him in about the picture on his phone and his driver's license. "But there's something about him. I can tell he's genuinely interested in the children."

"Or maybe in the support his brother pays you. Maybe he just wants the money." Daddy stood, paced the room—a trait they shared when unnerved. "It's a pretty penny. Some people would use it for themselves instead of strictly for the kids and socking everything that's left away for their future."

"I hope you're wrong." She hugged herself. The whole thing reminded her of Aunt Eleanor. "If he insists on inflicting himself into Mason and Madison's lives, I want him to love them."

"Me too."

But not in an obsessive way like Aunt Eleanor, who'd been so determined to raise Stacia and her sister, she'd tried to romance their dad, kidnapped them and fought for custody. They'd have to be on guard.

"Do you think it would be better if we told them before he gets here?"

The doorbell rang.

Stacia closed her eyes. "Unfortunately, I think that option is off the table."

"I'll get it." Daddy stood, ambled toward the front door, as if a rattlesnake waited on the other side.

Seconds later, male voices came from the foyer. Though their tones sounded cordial, Stacia couldn't make out their words.

What was up with that? She'd expected Daddy to be defensive, combative where Madison and Mason were concerned.

She hurried down the hall, popped her head into the guest room–turned–play area. Both children sat on the floor, contentedly building a large Lego structure.

"It's a dollhouse." Madison clicked more blocks into place.

"Uh-uh, it's a fort." Mason grabbed the Legos she'd just added and tugged them apart.

"Hey, none of that now," Stacia chastened. "Madison can pretend it's a dollhouse and you can pretend it's a fort."

"Or we could each build something different," Mason grumbled.

"As long as you do it happily. But right now, it's time for supper. And we have a guest."

"Who is it?" Madison piped up.

Someone who will change our lives forever.

Stacia's stomach churned. "Let's go see."

By the time she'd ushered the kids into the kitchen, Daddy and Ross were there waiting. And Daddy was smiling, like he'd made a new friend. Huh?

"We saw you in the store before." Mason sized Ross up.

"That's right." Ross looked as nervous as she felt.

"This is Mason and Madison." Her introduction came out forced.

"I'm Ross."

"Are you Aunt Stacia's boyfriend?" Madison giggled.

"Madison." Stacia shushed her niece as heat crept over her face.

"Actually, I'm here to see you guys." Ross knelt to their level.

"How come?" Mason scrunched his forehead.

"Because I'm your uncle."

Both children stared at Ross, wide-eyed.

"How?" Madison's gaze narrowed, as if cross-examining him. "Aunt Stacia doesn't have no brothers."

"Any brothers," Stacia corrected.

"Madison is all into sorting family out these days." Daddy chuckled.

Mason rolled his eyes.

"No eye rolling. Ross is your father's brother." Stacia's tone held no excitement.

"You know our father?" Mason, his interest obviously piqued, stepped closer to Ross.

"I do."

"Have you seen him lately?"

Stacia's breath stalled.

"Not too long ago." Ross glanced up at Stacia, trying to remember what the kids knew about Ron. All color had drained from her face. "I was passing through where he was working his job and he asked me to come and check on y'all."

"Really?" Madison stepped nearer. "Where was he?"

"I'm afraid that's classified. You know, since his job is so important."

"But he sent you to see about us?" Mason asked.

"He sure did. Because, even if his job is important, he wants to know y'all are okay."

"Then why doesn't he come see us?" Madison's chin quivered.

And if Ron were anywhere near, Ross would deck him.

"His boss won't let him." Stacia set one hand on each child's shoulder. "Remember, I told you."

"I wish he'd quit." Mason looked down at the floor. "I mean, I know he's important and all, but surely somebody else could do his job, so he could come home."

"Do you work with him?" Madison asked. "Is that why you're just now coming to see us?"

"I didn't know about y'all." Ross closed his eyes. "Until your dad asked me to apply for his job. But his boss didn't like me, so that's when your dad told me why he wanted to leave his job. Because of you two." As he added to Maverick's story, he understood the reasoning behind it. Five-year-olds shouldn't know their dad was into his career instead of them by choice.

"So I promised to make sure y'all were okay and to make sure you stay happy and healthy. So are you okay, happy and healthy?"

The twins nodded in unison.

"Except we can't remember our mom," Madison mumbled.

"Or our dad," Mason added.

"I'm sorry about that." Ross's chest squeezed. This was harder than he'd expected.

"That's why your mom left you with me." Stacia knelt

between them, hugged them to her sides. “So Grandpa and I can help you remember her. And because she knew we’d take extra good care of you.” Her gaze never left Ross.

“Aunt Stacia shows us pictures of our mom.” Mason wiggled out of the hug. “Do you have any pictures of our dad?”

Just the one. Of a pale, sickly looking Ron in character with blue hair and overdone eyeliner lying in a hospital bed. His publicist had insisted on doing his goth makeup before she’d allow any photos. Just in case the press ever got a hold of it. These two innocent bystanders, products of his brother’s wreck of a life, didn’t need to see that.

“I’m afraid not. But he looks a lot like me.” He used to anyway, before he changed into Ronny Outrageous.

“Okay, I think that’s enough questions.” Maverick clapped his hands. “How about that supper you promised this old grandpa?”

“On the table.” Stacia stood. “Just let me get ice in the glasses.”

Mason rubbed his stomach. “I’m starving.”

“Me too.” Ross’s gut growled to prove it.

“You can sit here.” Madison motioned to a chair with no plate or utensils. Obviously, Stacia had hoped he’d be a no-show.

“I’ll get the extra place setting.” Maverick hurried to a cabinet. “What do you want to drink, Ross?”

He eyed the tea pitcher as Stacia poured the amber liquid into four glasses.

“Tea sounds great.”

“It’s sweet.” Distrust glowed in Stacia’s eyes.

“Just the way I like it.” At least they were even since he didn’t trust her either. The difference was, he’d give her a chance to prove herself. Would she do the same? Or was she like his ex-girlfriend, Nora—incapable of trusting anyone?

* * *

The chicken enchilada sat untouched on Stacia's plate. It was usually one of her favorite meals, but not tonight. Not with Ross Lyles sitting across the table from her, chatting up the twins, endearing himself as their new-found uncle.

"Well that was delicious." Ross folded his napkin, set it beside his plate.

"Come build Legos with us, Uncle Ross."

Stacia's tea went down the wrong way. She grabbed a napkin, coughed into it, gasped and hacked her way back to a clear airway.

"You okay?" Ross asked. "I know the Heimlich."

Of course he did. He was perfect, already had the twins calling him uncle.

"I'm fine. I'm afraid it's almost bedtime for these two though."

"But Uncle Ross is here," Mason whined.

"We have church tomorrow. And if we get up early, we go to bed early. So go on, get your pajamas. I'll get the showers going."

"Can't Uncle Ross stay, Aunt Stacia? He could even tuck us in." Mason tried another tactic.

"Absolutely not." Stacia's nerve endings pinged, past keeping it together. "And remember the no whining rule."

"What your aunt means is she doesn't know me yet. But don't worry, I'm not going anywhere. In fact, I'm working here at the store and the ranch, so you'll see a lot of me."

"Yay." Madison headed for the stairs in the foyer.

"I got this." Daddy followed the twins. "Why don't you come to church with us tomorrow, Ross?"

Stacia shot Daddy a withering look, but he totally missed it.

"I just might do that."

It wasn't that she didn't want Ross at church. She just needed some space from him. But it was too late; her dad was giving him the church's name and address.

"I'll let you see our guest off, Stacia. Good night, Ross."

"Good night, Maverick."

"Good night, Uncle Ross." The twins echoed each other. And their new name for him made her want to scream.

"Let me help you clean up."

"That's really not necessary." She started for the door.

He didn't follow but gathered plates from the table. "I insist."

"I have a dishwasher."

"Then I'll help you load it."

"Fine." She rolled her eyes, opened the dishwasher.

He retrieved dishes while she raked leftovers into the disposal and loaded them in the rack.

"I think tonight went well." He set two glasses beside her.

"As easily as you lied to them, how do I know if you're even telling the truth about why you're here?"

"Back to that, are we? I don't consider it a lie when covering up the fact that their father totally doesn't care anything about them. If anything, he feels guilt." The sadness in his tone tugged at her. "And besides, your dad's the one who made up his oh-so-important job."

"Your brother's a real piece of work." She hugged herself. "Making us both cover up for him. No offense."

"None taken. Ron has always been selfish."

Did he really have such a harsh opinion of his brother, or was he only trying to tear down her defenses?

"What about your sister? What was she like?"

"Heartbroken. Our mom had a heart condition." She rinsed each dish before loading them in the dishwasher.

"Mom died when I was thirteen and Calli was eleven. She took it really hard and was never the same. She went from this fun, outgoing little girl who loved church to a sullen child who refused to go and looked for trouble at every turn." Which is when Aunt Eleanor came to stay with them and made everything even worse.

"Was she a good mother to the twins?"

"Calli's teens and twenties were completely reckless. Until the twins. Once she had them, she settled down, even started going to church with us again and accepted Jesus as her savior. She was a very devoted mother." Her voice broke. "They grounded her, reached the reasonable side of her when no one else could."

"She must have been terribly young when she died."

"Twenty-three. She had the same heart condition as our mom." Stacia blinked tears away. Even after three years, she couldn't talk about Calli and remain dry-eyed.

"I'm sorry."

"Thanks. Were you and your brother ever close?"

"When we were young." With the dishes cleared, he grabbed the soapy washcloth out of the sink and wiped down the table. "He was selfish then too, never wanted to share, always thought the world revolved around him. But I guess I did too, so we got along well. Until he started singing and people made a big deal over him. He sprouted an ego the size of Texas and we steadily grew apart."

"I'm sorry."

"Thanks." He helped her load the dishwasher. "It doesn't seem like you get much time with the kids in the evening."

"What's that supposed to mean?" Her eyes narrowed.

"By the time you close the store, it's time to prepare supper. Then once they eat, it's time to get them ready for bed."

"And you could do better?" Everything he said seemed to rub her the wrong way.

"That's not what I meant."

"Then what do you mean?"

"It was just an observation, that we live in such a busy world, I wish there was more time. Once I start at the store, I won't see them much." A tinge of longing echoed in his tone.

One she understood since she never seemed to have enough time with the kids now that they'd started kindergarten. Back in preschool, they'd gone only three days a week. She missed those years.

"Well before my store clerk married my ranch hand and moved to Waco, everything wasn't so busy around here." She jerkily scrubbed the baked-on cheese off the casserole dish. "Daddy and I took turns, spending alternating days with them, while the other worked in the shop. I'm hoping with you at the store, we can get back in that routine."

"Well, look who's getting along." Daddy stepped into the room, took his seat at the table.

"Just be glad you didn't show up a few minutes ago." Ross grinned.

Stacia ignored him. "Are they both bathed?"

"Yep, read them a story and they're down for the count."

Ross slid the last plate into the rack. "I better be going."

"Maybe not." Daddy scratched his chin. "I have an idea."

"What's that?" Ross asked.

"There's an apartment across from Stacia's workshop in the cattle barn. Used to be where our ranch hand lived. You could move in there if you don't mind a few moos and whinnies."

"Daddy. No."

But he ignored her. "It might need a deep cleaning, a little sprucing up, but it would save you some money and a commute if you're gonna be here every day."

"Absolutely not."

"What's gotten into you, Stacia?"

"What's gotten into you, Daddy? We don't know this guy." She waved her hand at Ross. "For all we know he could be a serial killer. And you're practically inviting him to move in with us."

Maverick turned to Ross. "I apologize for my daughter's rudeness."

"It's okay, I appreciate her caution when it comes to my niece and nephew."

Her gaze pinged back and forth between them, then landed on her dad. "Stop it, Daddy. You're supposed to take my side."

"I am on your side. But I'm on Madison and Mason's side too. This is their uncle. He has as much of a right to be part of their lives as we do. I'm trying to make the best of a difficult situation."

"By inviting a man we don't know to move in." She did a little fake shudder.

"Nonsense, Stacia." Daddy scoffed. "He's not moving into the house. And I've still got my gun."

"In that case—" Ross laughed "—maybe I should just go back to Bandera for the night."

"No you won't." Daddy pulled a key from the hook on the wall, handed it to Ross. "The place is yours for as long as you wanna stick around."

"I appreciate it. But I've already paid for my cabin, so I'll stay there tonight."

"After church tomorrow, if you'll come by, we can get the apartment cleaned up and move-in ready," Daddy suggested.

"Sounds like a plan."

So now he'd won over the twins and her dad. But not Stacia. She had to remain on high alert, in protective mode. The twins depended on her. And she wouldn't let this guy just waltz in, pull an Aunt Eleanor, and take them away from her. No matter how handsome he was.

Morning sunlight dappled the walls of Stacia's bedroom as she slipped earrings in, checked her reflection, then headed for the stairs. Just as Daddy came out of his room.

"You okay?" He touched her elbow.

"Where are the twins?"

"Downstairs."

"I feel like we're losing them," she whispered as moisture clouded her vision.

"We won't. I won't allow that to happen."

"And it's like you're taking Ross's side. When did y'all become best buds?"

"We can't afford to make this guy mad. He's got the upper hand, Stace." He put his arm around her shoulders, kissed the top of her head. "He could take us to court and with Ron's money to back him, that terrifies me. Even though your aunt lost when she tried it years ago, I've seen it on the news, too many kids ripped away from adoptive families because the birth family had a change of heart. I figure we play nice and try to compromise, rather than take the chance of losing everything."

"You're right." She blew out a big breath. "I'll try. But he just jerks all my nerve endings at the same time."

"God's got this. Let Him handle things when you can't."

As they descended the steps, the front door slammed.

"I told y'all to stay inside until time to leave for church," Daddy shouted.

No response.

"They've escaped in their church clothes." She hurried down the stairs and out the door after them. A squeal echoed as she stepped out on the porch.

"Make him stop, Aunt Stacia!" Madison screamed as she ran by.

Mason giggled, in hot pursuit of his twin sister, with both hands cupped around something.

"Mason, stop chasing your sister this instant or I'll ground you from the side-by-side."

That stopped him in his tracks.

"You're both supposed to be inside. What have you got?" Stacia dashed down the porch steps.

"A big ugly frog." Madison darted behind her. "He was gonna put it on me."

"Let me see it, big guy."

Mason headed toward her with a sly grin as Madison shot out from behind her and ran to the door. Before he even reached her, Stacia knew exactly what he planned to do. He opened his hands enough for her to see a large toad's head, then promptly set it on her arm.

She kept still, then gingerly caught the toad and held him in one hand.

"You didn't scream. Or run." Mason frowned.

"Because I'm not afraid of him. Come see, Madison."

"Nope."

"Frogs can't hurt you. And this is actually a toad. They like to be petted." She ran her finger down the toad's back.

"What's the difference?" Madison crept closer.

"Most frogs are slimy with smoother skin and their legs are longer with sticky feet. Toads have shorter legs and rougher, drier skin."

"Do they give you warts?" Mason ran his grubby finger down the toad's back.

"No. That's a myth."

"But they tinkle on you." Madison gagged.

"If you scare them. But not if you pick them up really gently like this." She gripped the toad between her finger and thumb. "Right behind his front legs, where his belly sticks out on each side. Really gently, just enough to hold him. That way if he tinkles, it's not on you. You let him get it out of his system and then set him in your hand."

A dark pickup turned into the drive, but she couldn't tell who was inside. The door opened and Ross climbed out. Obviously dressed for church, wearing a white shirt, black slacks and a tie.

"Uncle Ross." The twins bolted for him.

"Stop this instant!" Stacia shouted.

Both children stopped in their tracks.

"You'll get him dirty. Go wash your hands."

"A little dirt never hurt anybody." Ross beckoned them with both hands.

Mason took off, but Madison looked back at Stacia.

"Go ahead." She sighed.

Each twin hugged one of his legs until he knelt to their level and transferred their hugs to his neck.

"Come look at the toad I found." Mason let go and darted back in her direction.

Ross stood and Madison clasped his hand as he strolled toward her.

"Madison's afraid of him." Mason snickered.

"I am not. Not anymore. Aunt Stacia showed us how to pick them up, so they don't tinkle on you."

"A fine skill to have." Ross stepped close, inspected the toad. "And that's a mighty fine toad you've got there."

"I think I'll keep him." Mason stayed still while she passed the toad back to him.

"He might have a family and I bet they miss him," Ross said.

Something in his eyes made her realize he wasn't talking about the toad.

"I'll put him back where I found him."

"Do that, then come in to wash your hands and face." She gently tapped his nose with her finger. "No more scaring or chasing your sister and hurry, it's time to leave."

"Okay." Mason's tone sounded as if she'd just deflated all the fun out of his young life.

She shooed Madison inside. Once the door closed, she crossed her arms under her chest. "Nice line about the toad."

"That's what my mom always told me and Ron when we were kids and caught some critter or another."

"She sounds like a good mom."

"The best."

"So you're headed to church?"

"I thought I'd follow y'all, if that's okay?"

She couldn't begrudge him church. "Sure."

Mason returned from taking the toad to its home. "I hope his family finds him."

"I'm sure they will." Ross shot him a wink and Mason scurried through the door.

The door opened behind her and she turned to see Daddy.

"Ross. I can't remember the last time someone actually showed up when I invited them to church."

"I've gone my entire life, so I figure I should find a church home while I'm here."

Madison came back out. "We're waiting on Mason, as usual."

"We've still got time." Stacia checked her watch.

"We always have to wait on Mason." Madison rolled her eyes.

"No eye rolling. Especially about your brother." Though

Stacia's tone was kind, she gave the little girl a chastening look.

Daddy made small talk about the church as minutes ticked by until Mason returned.

"You're coming to church with us?" Mason grinned.

"Sure am." Ross did a fist bump with the child. "Want to ride with me?"

If he got the kids in his truck, he could disappear with them. Just like Aunt Eleanor had all those years ago.

"No!" The single word dripped all the panic that clenched Stacia's heart. "I mean, we can't all fit in there and we'd have to move their car seats. You can follow us."

"Or he could ride with us," Daddy said. "There's plenty of room in your SUV with its third-row seating."

She closed her eyes, stole a deep breath. Like it or not, Ross wasn't going away. And she didn't like it. Not one bit.

Maverick pulled into the church lot, and Ross opened the passenger door as soon as the SUV stopped rolling. He'd enjoyed the other man's easy conversation and Mason and Madison's constant chatter.

But even with Stacia in the back seat, her strawberry scent had distracted him the entire ten-minute drive. Not in a cloying, allergy-inducing way. But in an unmistakably feminine manner and he was more than eager to escape it. She very well might be the enemy and he couldn't afford to find her attractive. No matter how beautiful she was.

Besides that, she was bent on mistrusting him and he needed to wrap up this mission and get back to Houston.

"Come to Sunday school class with us." Mason unfastened his car seat and bailed out, grabbing Ross's hand and tugging him toward the church.

"I'm afraid your uncle is an adult." Stacia clutched her

Bible against her heart, like a shield. "He can't go to your class."

"But Rance and Larae are adults and they're in my class."

"They're your teachers or they'd be in the adult class."

"You'll see Uncle Ross during the church service." Maverick herded the group toward the building. "Maybe you can sit by him."

"That will never work." Stacia grumbled. "The kids have to sit between us or they won't be still and quiet."

Obviously she planned to fight him every step of the way. Was she being protective or did she have something to hide? Was she worried the children might out her on some sort of abuse or neglect if they got too close to him?

Inside the lobby, Maverick introduced him to the pastor, a baby-faced man though the graying in his temples revealed he was probably in his forties.

"Y'all go on to class." Stacia hugged each twin.

They waved bye to him and dashed down a long corridor.

"No running."

Their steps slowed.

"Don't you need to walk them to class?"

"It's just the fourth door down. And I trust my church family." Her gaze shot darts.

Message relayed, loud and clear: he was the only one she didn't trust.

A man stepped from the fourth door down, greeted the twins.

"Who's that?"

"That's Rance Shepherd." Maverick led him down the hall. "He's married to Stacia's best friend, Larae. Good stock with a truckload of biblical knowledge. The twins have memorized countless Bible verses this year with him and Larae as their teachers. Our class is this way." The older man stopped, turned back. "Aren't you coming?"

Stacia stood in the entry. "I'm working the nursery."

"It's not your week." Maverick frowned. "Is it?"

"No." Her pale face turned blotchy red. "But I heard Mrs. Johnson is sick, so I thought I'd see if they need help."

In other words, to avoid Ross. Worked for him; he'd had enough of her strawberry presence.

Maverick continued down the hall, turned into a classroom where a man and woman were seated at the front of the room with rows of chairs facing them.

"Denny, Stella, y'all doing okay this fine morning?"

"Just fine. How about yourself, Maverick?" Denny shook his hand.

"Can't complain. Not too much anyway."

A veiled complaint about Ross.

"Maverick, always the first to show." Stella stood and hugged him. "And you brought a guest."

"This is Ross Lyles. He's staying at the ranch for a bit, helping with the store and the cattle."

"It's nice to meet you." Stella offered her hand as Denny did the same.

"Ross, meet Denny and Stella Parker. Their daughter, Lexie, is friends with Stacia."

"Nice to meet you both." Frustration bottled up in his chest. He wanted to clarify, tell these people that he was the twins' uncle. But apparently Maverick wanted to keep that bit of news private. He'd let it ride, for now.

Other church members filed in. Couples and apparent singles, from young adults to grandparents. Maverick introduced him to each person and he promptly forgot every single name. Except for Lexie and her fiancé, Clint, since the former had been pointed out as friends of Stacia. Anyone connected with her—or the twins—piqued his interest.

The study was in-depth on Romans, one of Ross's favorite books of the Bible. He lost all sense of time and worries as Denny and Stella tag teamed the topic with frequent questions and discussion from the class. As an older gentleman closed in prayer, Ross had to admit, so far hc really liked this church.

As people spilled out of the classroom, Ross thanked the teachers for a well-thought-out, obviously studied lesson.

"Grandpa." Two small voices blended together as the twins squeezed through the sea of people leaving.

"I didn't know Uncle Ross came to class with you." Mason piped up. "You're old and he's not."

Ross suppressed a chuckle. "Your grandfather isn't old and besides he's young at heart."

The room had gone silent. It hit Ross why. Mason had called him *Uncle*. Two sets of wary Parker eyes rested on him. It was obvious from Denny and Stella's stricken stares, they knew who the twins' father was.

A few others had apparently heard, but theirs were only curious glances his way before leaving the room.

"We better get to the sanctuary." Maverick hustled him out the door.

Maybe Maverick hadn't explained who he was because anyone who knew the twins' parentage wouldn't welcome him with open arms.

Chapter Three

As soon as Stacia entered the sanctuary, her friend Lexie pounced on her. "So who's the cute guy you brought to church with you? Are you dating him?"

"That would be a hard no." A sigh emanated from Stacia. "You won't believe who he is."

Larae entered, joined their circle. The swell of her pregnant belly always put an ache in Stacia's heart.

"Madison told me in class that their uncle is here. But she doesn't have any uncles. But since she calls me and Lexie aunt sometimes, I figure he's a friend. But then I got a load of Mr. Tall, Dark and Handsome with your dad." Larae thumped Stacia's shoulder. "I can't believe you're seeing someone and you didn't tell us."

"Trust me, I'm not seeing him. We only met yesterday and he's their biological uncle."

"Wait, you don't have a brother, do you?" Lexie's confusion stamped a crease between her eyebrows.

"Their father's brother."

Her friends' gasps echoed each other, followed by their joint, "Noooo!"

"I'm afraid it's true."

"But Ronny *Ridiculous* doesn't have any family," Lexie insisted.

"That's what he told me. Obviously he lied."

Larae's eyes turned steely. "Did he give you any proof? He could be some reporter. Or a blackmailer."

"I thought the same thing. I saw proof." She filled them in on Ronny's estrangement from his family and then confession to his brother after his accident.

"What does he want?" Lexie bit her lip.

"He claims he wants to get to know the twins. For now."

"He can't take them from you, can he?" Larae clutched her arm.

"I don't know." She closed her eyes.

Both friends hugged her.

"We won't let that happen," Larae promised. "I'll get you the best lawyer."

Larae was the sole heir to her parents' deep pockets. On top of that, she owned a profitable rodeo. Her friend never threw her wealth around and Stacia didn't believe in handouts, but this was different.

"If it comes to that, I'll take you up on it." Stacia's voice quivered.

Her friends stayed by her side as they made their way to their pews. But Stacia kept going. Straight to the altar. Before the service even started, she knelt.

"I can't do this, Lord," she whispered. "I can't lose them. I know it's selfish. Their grandparents have a right to know them, but please don't let them take the twins away from me. Take all my worries, ease my anxiety, give me peace. And fix this for me. Please. In Jesus' precious name, Amen."

She stood, noticed Ross kneeling a few feet away. Stunned, she forced herself to return to her seat beside her niece. At least he was a Christian. The knowledge settled her nerves.

Minutes passed and Ross stood, came to their pew, started to sit by her dad.

"Sit between me and Mason, Uncle Ross." Madison patted the pew. "That way Mason's sitting by Grandpa, so we're still between y'all, but we get to sit by Uncle Ross too."

Despite his presence, peace swept through her. Only the kind God could give.

Their eyes met and a silent acknowledgment passed between them. They were on the same page spiritually. All they had to do was act like it, get along in a civil manner and do whatever was best for the twins. Surely he could see that Madison and Mason needed to remain in the only home they'd ever known.

Only time would tell. She needed to show her best, sweetest, nurturing side. Easy when it came to the twins. But when it came to him, not so much. She'd certainly do her level best to kill his worries with kindness. If she had to bite her tongue off to do it.

Unsure if she hadn't heard him enter the workshop or was ignoring him, Ross watched as Stacia ran the wire brush attachment on her drill over a stubborn rust spot that refused to relinquish its hold on the exterior side of the tub.

After church yesterday, her dad had helped him clean the apartment, while she'd taken the twins for a ride in the woods on their four-seater side-by-side. Her only contribution had been freshly laundered sheets. Maverick had invited him to supper as well and she'd obviously been uncomfortable during the meal, picking at her food.

Finally, the corrosion came loose and melted away into

dust. She turned off the drill, pulled her goggles up on top of her head and ran her hand over the iron.

"What should I tackle?" he asked.

Stacia squealed, dropped her drill.

"Sorry." He picked up the power tool, pulled the trigger to make sure it still worked, then set it on her worktable. "The door was open and I thought you'd be expecting me."

"Not this early." She clutched her hand to her chest. "You almost gave me a heart attack. The twins haven't even left for kindergarten yet."

"I was hoping to see them before they leave. I went to the house first, rang the bell, but didn't get an answer."

"Daddy probably thought it was a delivery and I'd handle it. He's getting the twins ready and driving them to school this morning. We take turns."

Maybe someday, he could have a turn. But not anytime soon from the looks of her. Despite their Christian bond at church yesterday, today the wariness in her eyes had returned.

"You look like a cartoon character with those goggles on your head."

Her face reddened. "Glamour doesn't usually hang around in the workshop."

"You don't need glamour." If they weren't on opposite sides of the issue, he could easily get caught up in her beauty. He cleared his throat. "I feel like we made progress yesterday, that you at least found a reason to trust me."

"I'm trying to."

"Truce?" He offered his hand.

"Truce." She clasped it and electricity shot up his arm.

That first day, he'd noticed a smattering of coppery freckles splashed across her fair nose and cheeks. But yesterday and this morning, there was no trace of them. Fascinating, along with her aqua eyes a man could lose himself in and auburn hair with honeyed highlights that begged for fingers to run through the silky lengths.

He needed to get to work. "So do you want me to help with the tub?"

"I've got it."

"I'm not good at sitting around waiting. And I'm here to work."

"Okay. Since you're good at building furniture, you can start on the coffee bars. Each of those are a complete set." She pointed behind her where several old doors leaned with cellophane bags on the doorknobs of each. "The spindles and corbels are in the bags. The plywood is over there, some already ready. The rest can be cut to fit with a router to round the edges. Are you familiar with coffee bars?"

"Just the one in your store, but I think I can envision what you have in mind." He picked a door and went to work.

"They basically have a table with a shelf underneath the same size as the top, the corbels go under a thin shelf at the top." She picked up a tablet, scrolled down and showed him some examples. "If you'll assemble them, I'll handle the primer and paint, along with the corbels for the shelf and hooks to line each side of the door to hang coffee cups. They go on last."

"Got it." He stood the door against the work table, took the parts and pieces she'd gathered out of the bag and lined them up along with the screws she'd supplied. "Did you come up with the idea for these?"

"I wish. I saw one in another store and tweaked the design." Her face scrunched up as she sneezed.

"Bless you."

"Thanks. Sometimes the dust gets to me." She grabbed her sander, went back to work on the tub. "What type of furniture do you build for your parents' store?"

"Anything wood." He spoke loud enough for her to hear over the buzz of her tool. "Rocking chairs, headboards, log furniture. Their store specializes in cabin furniture."

"Really?" Apparently satisfied with her work, she set the sander down. "There's a store like that in Medina and one in Bandera, about fifteen minutes away. I love browsing there. How did your folks get into that?"

"My grandmother had a store similar to yours and my dad worked for her." Ross chuckled at the memory her question brought up. "But the furniture store started when Dad found a cypress stump. He thought it would make a nice tenth anniversary gift for my mom since she likes unique pieces. He created an end table by cutting it to stand level and securing a live edge slab on top. She loved it.

"Until a month later, we were watching a movie on TV when I noticed a tiny praying mantis on my arm." He inspected the coffee bar Maverick had built to see how the parts were attached. Looked like he'd built the table first. "Then Dad saw one on the couch and mom found one on her chair. There were eggs in the stump. The mantises had hatched and were crawling out in droves."

"Oh no." She shivered, obviously imagining the sea of tiny green bugs. "What did they do?"

"He set the table on the back porch for a week to make sure they'd all evacuated, then he sealed the stump." He sank a screw to attach a spindle to the router-edged plywood that would serve as the table top. "Friends and family loved it and wanted him to build them tables, so he did. He learned to let stumps sit on the porch for at least six months before sealing them. He'd found his passion and several stores started selling his creations.

"Then one of them offered him a job in Houston, so we

moved there. Eventually, the owner retired and my folks bought the business."

The buzz of her air compressor started up and they fell into silence as they worked. Not companionable like it was when he worked with his dad. Every nerve ending he possessed was on high alert, all too aware of her presence.

True to her word, Stacia made nice in the workshop, until her head was about to explode.

She'd never appreciated the racket the compressor made, but today, it was her favorite thing. As long as the rumble filled the air, she could pretend Ross wasn't there. Or maybe pretend to pretend. She'd been in such a tizzy about the twins, she honestly hadn't thought a whole lot about his looks. Until Lexie had pointed it out yesterday.

His hair was longer than most cowboys, with curls flipping every which way. Paired with grass-green eyes that seemed to look straight through you. With today being the first time she'd been alone with him, the handsome cowboy was hard to ignore.

The air tank kicked off, launching them into silence. An uncomfortable silence.

With the bathtub stripped of rust, she put on a mask and handed him one. "I'll be spraying primer, so put this on."

He obeyed. If only the mask would cover those eyes.

"If you'll assemble the coffee bars, I'll do the painting."

"I understand why you keep the doors open."

"It gets pretty smothery in the summer, but at least we're past the hottest days of the year." She swiped the back of her hand over her sweaty forehead. Great, just what she needed, a great-looking guy in her workshop watching her freckles appear one by one as her makeup melted away and her hair turned into a frizzy mess.

But what did she care? He was Madison and Mason's uncle. Her opponent, even if he was a Christian. She couldn't afford to find him attractive. Not when she might be in for the fight of her life. No consorting with the enemy. She turned on the sprayer and focused on the bathtub.

"Smells like progress in here." Daddy stepped in the back door. "The twins are successfully delivered on time."

"You need a nap after that." Stacia chuckled and stopped painting until Maverick slipped a mask on.

"No naps for the weary. Too many coffee bars to be built."

"Morning, Maverick." Ross set down his screwdriver. "The cattle are all fed and accounted for."

"See, he's paying off already." Daddy shot her a wink, then got to work on constructing a coffee bar. "Can you paint, Ross? With a sprayer?"

"I can."

"Another point in your favor. I've never mastered the sprayer. I drip more than a teething toddler."

With Daddy in the workshop making small talk, Stacia could breathe better. Despite the paint fumes.

But the reprieve didn't last long. By the time she'd finished priming the tub, it was time for Daddy to tend the store.

And her breathing hitched again. The rest of the day passed with the buzz of power tools interspersed with small talk. Her only reprieve from him was when she ran to the house to make sandwiches for lunch. Then afterward, Stacia took Ross through the steps of reglazing a bathtub until the door from the store opened and the twins blasted inside.

"Uncle Ross," their two voices echoed as they flocked him.

Stacia's heart took a dive. "Y'all are supposed to check

if it's okay for you to come in, remember?" At least the fumes had tamed.

"Sorry." Madison hung her head. "I forgot. We were excited cuz Grandpa said Uncle Ross was here."

"Can you play with us, Uncle Ross?" Mason asked. "Pleeeease."

Ross caught her gaze, as if asking permission.

"Not today." She set down her drill. "We'll need to do chores and homework and your uncle has work to do."

"Awww!" The twins' disappointment echoed one another.

"Tonight, after Grandpa and Uncle Ross finish with the cattle and the workshop, you can spend some time with him."

"Yay!" Madison and Mason jumped up and down.

"But for now, you get me." She ushered them toward the exit.

No yays about spending time with her. Her stomach sank further. It wasn't so much jealousy. It downright hurt.

As morning daylight filled the kitchen, Stacia hurriedly ate at the breakfast bar.

"What's got you so down in the mouth?" Daddy strode into the room, always attuned to her moods.

"I'm okay."

"No, you're not. Spill."

"The kids are so excited to spend time with Ross. I mean, I'm glad they like him since he's their uncle and he's not going anywhere. But—"

"You wish they were that excited about us."

"I'm a bad aunt." Her face warmed.

"No, you're not. You've poured the last three years of your life into them." He gave her shoulder a squeeze. "Remember how they were all about Larae when she first moved back to Medina? And then they were all about Lexie when she moved back. Ross is just someone new and exciting in their world. He'll become part of the scenery before you know it."

If he didn't end up taking them back to Houston with him.

"I hope so." She downed the last of her pineapple juice and headed toward the foyer. "I better go corral them."

"I'm off to the workshop."

Halfway up the stairs, giggles erupted from Madison's room. She sped up to see what mischief they'd gotten into. And promptly interrupted a pillow fight between the children as they smacked each other with fluffy cushions.

Her heart warmed, as she remembered her own such antics with their mother in this very room. "Okay, break it up. It's almost time to go."

Madison dropped her pillow, but Mason got one more shot in before doing the same. Just like Calli used to.

"Have you brushed your teeth?"

"Yes." Their voices blended.

"Go brush your hair."

"We already did," Mason said.

"It looks like that was before the pillow fight." She tousled his disheveled hair.

While Madison was all about lingering hugs and sitting in Stacia's lap, Mason was too impatient and squirmy. She'd learned to get creative in ways of showing her affection with him.

"Can you French braid mine?" Madison handed her a brush and pony holder.

"Sure." Stacia sat down on the edge of the bed as Madison turned her back to stand in front of her. She separated the thick red locks into three sections.

"Where does Uncle Ross live?" the little girl asked.

"In Houston."

"How long is he staying here?"

"I'm not sure."

Mason returned from the bathroom. "I hope he stays forever."

"Wow, that's a long time." Stacia was torn. She'd love for Ross to go away, to not complicate the twins' lives or custody situation. But if he grew bored with playing uncle and abandoned them, her niece and nephew would be hurt. And if he was sincere about being a fixture in their world, he might very well take Mason and Madison away from her.

Please Lord, fix this, where no one gets hurt. Especially not the twins.

"It's time to go." Madison, the rule follower, a child after her own heart.

"All done." Stacia twisted the holder into place. "Race you downstairs."

Mason darted out of the room. Thankfully, he fell for her hurrying him up trick every time and never noticed she and Madison didn't even try.

"Uncle Ross!" Mason's excited shout echoed up the stairs.

What was he doing here so early?

Halfway down, she caught a glimpse of Ross and stopped short.

Framed by the fireplace with the ornate mantle her mom had begun to restore, he squatted to hug Mason, then looked up, smiled.

She tried to return the greeting, but her lips refused to tip up.

"Your dad invited me in for coffee."

"I see that." She descended the remaining steps.

Madison ran to him and got her hug. Then he stood,

hatless and barefoot, retrieved his porcelain mug and took a sip. Looking way too at home.

"I didn't figure you'd want my barnyard boots in your house and when I was taking them off outside, I made a mess of my socks." He scrunched his nose, then turned to the fireplace. "This is a great piece."

"Thanks. My mom found it at an estate sale. She started restoring it, but didn't get to finish. So Daddy and I did." Her voice caught. They'd painstakingly cleaned and polished every spindle and shelf until it shone, as a memorial to her.

"That tiger scares me." Madison pointed at the bronze tiger ready to pounce, crouching on the mantle.

"This guy." Ross ran his hand along the statue's back. "He's harmless. Have you ever petted him?"

Madison shook her head.

"Come on, give it a try." Ross reached for her and she allowed him to pick her up. Level with the tiger, she tentatively touched it, then stroked it's back.

"He's still scary looking."

"Agreed. But he's all cold, hard bronze. Even his teeth."

"I like the deer." Mason straddled the huge vintage brass stag reclining at the foot of the fireplace.

"Careful, don't let him *buck* you off," Ross deadpanned.

Sending both twins into giggles.

Stacia had to admit, he was good with the children. But she was tired of all the bonding.

"We need to get to school."

"Can Uncle Ross take us?" Madison clung to him.

Absolutely not. He might be good with kids and a Christian. But she still didn't trust him enough to let him drive the kids to school without kidnapping them. Or even wrecking them.

"How about I ride with y'all?" He offered a compromise.

"Yay!" Both kids whooped.

"Where are your backpacks?" Stacia clapped her hands to spur them into action.

"Upstairs." The twins' voices blended.

"Go get them. Make it back in two minutes and you can have a double scoop of ice cream after school."

Madison and Mason scurried up the staircase.

"I've seen mantles like this with a five-thousand-dollar price tag." Ross was still eyeing the fireplace. "Unless I'm mistaken, the tiger is from the Japanese Meiji period and well worth a few thousand, and the stag is Sarreid over fifteen hundred. I'd have to research the antique doll, but I'm certain it's worth a pretty penny as well."

"How do you know all that?" They were like kindred spirits. Only they couldn't be.

"I told you my grandmother owns a flea market/antique shop in Hondo. I'm a certified antiquities appraiser."

"That's something you could have mentioned."

"I didn't think about it. It's not like I filled out an application or even supplied my résumé."

"I probably need to get one of those, just for our books." And to do a background check. "I'll get you an application today. Which antique store in Hondo?"

"Grandpappy's Fleas & Tiques."

"Myrna is your grandmother?" Warmth she felt for Myrna softened her voice. Surely with a gem for a grandmother, he must be okay. But then Ronny Outrageous—twin abandoner extraordinaire—was his brother.

"You know her?"

"I shop her store. Often. And I miss her since she retired."

"She may not run the store anymore, but she spends

her time online finding pieces for it and dawdling about with Papaw on their ranch."

"She's a sweetheart. I can't believe she's your grandmother."

His gaze narrowed, as if he were pondering. "I'm not sure how to take that."

"I just meant it's a small world." But for the twins' sake, the results on the background check they ran on all employees needed to come back clean.

"That it is." He ran his hand over the mantle. "Why don't you sell them?"

"My mom got the whole setup at an estate sale. Back when she first opened the business. She had no idea what they were worth. Apparently, neither did the auctioneer or the family who sold them. I think she paid three hundred for the whole deal." She'd cleaned and polished the mantle until her final heart attack.

"Once she did her research, she felt horrible and tried to contact the family, but they were military and she never could catch up with them. So she decided if the family couldn't profit from what was rightfully theirs, she wouldn't either. It was the last piece she worked on before… Daddy and I finished it." Her gaze glossed over at the painful memories. "We keep it as a memorial and a testament of her character."

"It must have been really hard on you, losing her as a young teen."

"Yes." She hated it when he was all sympathetic and almost likeable.

But like it or not, Ross was the twins' uncle. They were growing to love him. Even if she refused to.

The twins scurried down the stairs.

She swallowed hard and checked her watch. "Great job. We better get a move on."

* * *

A few minutes later, with both twins secured in their booster seats, Stacia pulled out of the driveway.

Ross felt odd, being chauffeured.

"Do you think Uncle Ross could bring us to school, sometime?" Mason asked.

Stacia almost visibly cringed. "I'll have to get to know him better and make sure he's a good driver first."

"By that time, school will be out," Mason muttered.

She laughed. "It's only September."

"It took you forever to agree when I wanted to go to Bobby's house. You had to meet his parents and ask around for months before I got to go."

"Sounds like your aunt is watching out for you." Ross defended her. "But I can assure you, I don't have any tickets or outstanding warrants for my arrest," he quipped.

"Good to know."

"Can he eat supper with us again soon?"

"How about we slow down a bit?" Ross tugged at the seatbelt cutting into his shoulder. "We don't want to wear out my welcome. Give your aunt a chance to get used to me. I'm not going anywhere." If they made a habit of taking the kids to school together, maybe eventually she'd trust him enough to at least let him drive. He needed to get car seats for his truck, just in case.

"Grandpa's taking us to the park after school." Mason squirmed, loosened his seat belt a bit. "Can you come with us, Uncle Ross?"

"We'll see." A resounding yes danced on the tip of his tongue, but he needed to clear things with their aunt, once they were alone.

"Do you have any kids, Uncle Ross?" Madison asked.

"Not yet. But I hope to get married and have some one day."

The rest of the short trip passed as the twins peppered him with questions and invitations. Even though he'd not accepted any of them, he could almost see Stacia's hackles rising with each one.

She pulled into the drop-off line and inched along. A man and two women patrolled the sidewalk, making sure the kids got out safely and headed straight for the building. When they got close enough, the man opened the back door.

"Morning Mason, Madison. Good to see you, Stacia." He scrutinized Ross through the passenger window, then peered past him attempting to make eye contact with her.

Making Ross's hackles rise. Why did he care if this guy liked her?

"Morning, Principal Caruthers." Stacia kept her gaze on the rearview mirror as the twins clambered out of the back seat and said their goodbyes.

The man's mouth tightened.

"I'll see y'all after school." Ross waved.

"Have a good day." Principal Caruthers shut the car door, then tore his gaze away from her long enough to watch until the twins were inside.

The cars in front of them had emptied of kids and moved forward.

"For the last two years, I parked and walked them into preschool." Stacia followed the line of vehicles back onto the highway. "Once they're in kindergarten, everything changes. They're growing up so fast."

And on top of that, she dealt with the principal pining for her every morning. "Is it just me, or does the principal have a thing for you?"

"Adrian and I dated a few years back. He wanted kids and I—" her voice broke "—things fell apart when I got the twins. He wanted his own kids, not someone else's."

Ross wanted to say more. To tell her the guy was a jerk. That she deserved better. But she was obviously struggling with keeping her emotions in check and he didn't want to make it harder on her with sympathy.

So Adrian Caruthers broke up with her only to make eyes at her in the drop-off line. And Stacia obviously wasn't over him either, even if he was a jerk. Within minutes, they were back at the ranch. With the cattle tended to earlier and Maverick in the store, Ross went straight to the workshop.

"About all those invitations the twins offered, thanks for not accepting without us discussing it." She hesitated a moment. "It's okay with me for you to go to the park this afternoon. If you want."

"I definitely want. Thanks."

"Once the store is closed, we'll swap. I'll head to the park and you can finish up in the workshop this evening." She dug around in her desk, laid a form on top. "Here's an application. Something you usually need to fill out before getting hired."

"I'll fill it out tonight."

"Just so you know, we also run background checks on all of our employees. Something we usually do before we hire."

"Go for it. I've got nothing to hide." He could almost build a coffee bar with his eyes closed. Leaving his mind free to ponder. Maybe he could help Stacia out with her lost love. If he took the kids off her hands at least part of the time, she could take her life off Pause. If Adrian could handle part-time twins, Stacia would be free to resume her past relationship with him if she wanted.

Why did the thought put a pang in Ross's heart? Because Stacia deserved better than the creepy, selfish principal? Yeah, that was it.

Chapter Four

The day in the workshop had been long and tense. Ross was always glad to get a break. With the twins, his stress drained away. The park was just what he needed.

"Spin us, Uncle Ross," Madison called as they darted for the playground equipment. The twins clambered onto the merry-go-round. But their friend hung back a bit.

What was her name? Belonged to Stacia's friends Larae and Rance. He'd met them all at church.

"Hop on, Jayda." He remembered just in the nick of time.

She stepped onto the colorful tilting wheel lined with bars. A bit shy with him, she hadn't said much since they'd picked her up.

"Hold on really tight." Ross grabbed a bar and trotted around the whirligig.

"Faster," Mason shouted.

"Really, really tight." The three children clung to the rails as he sped up, then jumped on to join them. The surface wobbled with his weight. "Wow, I haven't done this in years. Why don't adults do this?"

"You're silly, Uncle Ross." Madison giggled.

His head spun. "I'm getting dizzy. Maybe this is why."

More giggling with Mason joining in.

The merry-go-round began to slow and Ross caught a glimpse of Stacia getting out of her car. With each spin, she was nearer. And angrier.

She stopped five feet away, propped her hands on her hips.

"Spin it fast again, Uncle Ross," Mason squealed.

"You got it." He jumped off, spun them faster and faster, but this time he didn't get back on. Instead he turned to face Stacia. She had the evil eye down to a science.

"Get on with us," Madison said.

"I think I need to talk to your aunt."

She turned and stalked toward where Maverick sat at a picnic table.

With no choice, Ross followed like a whipped pup and she hadn't even said anything yet. What had he done to rile her so?

"What were you thinking, Daddy?"

Maverick looked as if he were at a loss too. "About what?"

"You're way over here with Ross a mile away. He could have taken off with Mason and Madison and you couldn't have stopped him."

"I can assure you the thought never crossed my mind." Ross blew out an exasperated sigh.

"You're being ridiculous, hon." Maverick shook his head. "Ross isn't going to make off with the kids. And if he'd tried, I'm right here."

"Right here, a mile away with a bum knee."

"It's more like a hundred yards." Ross jabbed his thumb in his chest. "And I'm right here. Take this up with me. I offered to play with the kids and let your dad sit in the shade."

"Of course you did. You're intent on stealing them from me. Emotionally to begin with and then physically."

"Where is this coming from? If I'd wanted to take them and run, I'd have done it by now." His hands fisted at his sides. The chatter and chirp of birds, once peaceful, turned into a cacophony overhead as he worked at controlling his temper.

"Just go back to the workshop. You can come for supper tomorrow night and have properly supervised time with them."

"You're being ridiculous."

"I can be as ridiculous as I want. I have custody." She jabbed a thumb in her chest, obviously mocking him. "I'm responsible."

"Fine." He turned to check on the twins.

The merry-go-round had stopped. All three kids stood still, watching.

"Sorry guys." He waved. "I have to go back to the workshop. But your aunt Stacia will spin you and I'll see you tomorrow."

"Aw, bummer," the twins voices blended.

He turned back to face Stacia. "Just so you know, you're not hurting me. You're hurting them." He stalked to his truck.

"Spin us, Aunt Stacia," Madison called.

"I'll be there in a minute." Even with Ross long gone, Stacia was still steaming and needed to calm down before she could play.

"If you treat him that way, he's liable to take you to court." Daddy stood, started toward the merry-go-round.

A chill went down her spine. "I can't play nice and twiddle my thumbs while he steals them right from under us."

"I can spin it." Jayda hopped off, grabbed a rail and ran in circles.

"Just be careful," Stacia said.

"I will."

Daddy reclaimed his seat. "Ross is a Christian, Stace. And even if he wasn't, I was watching the whole time. He couldn't have gotten far."

"I can just see you hobbling after him."

"I do not hobble, thank you very much." Daddy's tone turned highly insulted.

"You do if you step in a hole and this place is full of them."

"Sweetheart, Ross is not your aunt Eleanor. He's not scheming, manipulative and obsessed."

"How would you know? You've known him for like a whole five minutes." She closed her eyes, trying hard to tamp down her frustration. "You always trust too fast."

"At least I trust. I knew what your aunt was up to. Within a week of her coming to live with us. I didn't know how she'd go about it, but I knew she wanted my girls."

"How?"

He shrugged. "I've always been good at reading people. Ross reads honest, caring and on the up-and-up."

"We'll see."

"We can't live constantly on guard. We can't anticipate everything in this life. You need to stop thinking you're in control. Trust God to keep the kids safe."

"I can't." She blinked tears away. She'd trusted God to keep Mama and Calli safe. She still trusted Him. With her life and eternity. Just not with the ones she loved most.

"I hope you'll pray about that. And in the meantime, if you're hostile toward Ross, the kids may take his side. He's the new exciting thing in their world and they knew you were mad at him just now. It's amazing what they pick up on."

"I'm aware." She bolted toward the merry-go-round, eager to escape the conversation.

"Ready for a spin?" She grabbed the bar as the rotation slowed.

"How come you made Uncle Ross leave?" Mason frowned.

Her breath caught. "I didn't."

"Yes you did." Madison scrutinized her. "You were mad at him."

"Not really mad." She tried to cover. "We just disagreed over a project in the workshop, so Ross left to fix it."

"Why don't you like him?" Mason persisted.

"I don't really know him very well yet."

"We do and we love him. We want you to love him too." Madison's voice held a lilt of sadness, as if Stacia had let her down.

Putting a hitch in her chest. "He's not my uncle, so I'm not really supposed to love him like y'all do." This conversation was worse than the one she'd fled from with Daddy.

"But you said Jesus wants us to love everybody, right?"

"You're right, Mad. I'll work on that." And for their sakes, she would. But she'd still be like a guard dog on patrol whenever he was with the twins.

"Spin us some more," Mason pleaded.

Stacia poured all her anger into the merry-go-round. She'd kill Ross with kindness. But no one would ever take them away from her, no matter what she had to do to stop them.

"That's fifteen coffee bars and fourteen completed bathtubs almost ready to be shipped." Stacia tucked a stray, russet tendril behind her ear.

Matter-of-fact, as if nothing had transpired between them at the park.

"I'm confused," Ross admitted. "Weren't we at each other's throats just last night?"

"About that. I thought about things, and we need to get along. For Mason's and Madison's sakes."

"Agreed."

"They knew we were arguing yesterday and that's not good. My bad and it won't happen again. At least not in front of the twins." She turned a withering glare on him. "But rabid Stacia will show up again if you try anything funny with them."

"Trust me, I'm well aware, but I don't have any devious plans."

"Good. We need to focus on production. If we stay on track with five of each per day, we'll make the deadline with no problem. And we get ahead of our quota when Daddy's here."

Working with her for the last few days, he'd solved the mystery of her now you see 'em, now you don't smattering of coppery freckles across her fair nose and cheeks. As each day wore on, she wiped dust or sweat away, until they appeared. It always made him wonder why she tried to cover them up.

His fingertips itched with the urge to count them. Stop staring. "How do you ship them?"

"Sometimes the salvage guys from Daddy's business make deliveries for us. But most of the time, we employ kids from the community college in Kerrville or the Bible college in Comfort to deliver for us on Saturdays. By the time they get their degree or find something else, word of mouth gets us a fresh crew."

"This place runs like a well-oiled machine."

"We've spent years working out the kinks."

"Oh, I almost forgot. I gave your dad my job application."

"If you've got any skeletons, they're about to come out."

"I'm not worried."

They'd fallen into a routine. In the mornings Ross tended the cattle and helped Maverick with the task in the evenings. During the day he worked in the workshop with Stacia. When the kids got home from school, Stacia or her dad watched them until the store closed. On slow days or when both clerks were there, Maverick helped in the workshop too.

Once the store was closed and the cattle was tended, he got to spend time with the twins at the ranch with Stacia's supervision while her dad went back to the workshop for a few more hours. Determined the B and B order wouldn't cut into family time, Stacia was careful not to work late at the store.

Ross's favorite times were in the evenings with her and the twins. After she'd wigged out at the park yesterday, he'd worried that might change. Thankfully, it seemed that wouldn't be the case.

The door from the store opened and Maverick stepped through. "Did you check your email, Stacia?"

"Not yet."

"Got a message from Bandera and Fredericksburg about the tubs and coffee bar parts you inquired about."

"Wonderful." She sat down at the computer.

"Tomorrow, you two make a bathtub, coffee bar run."

"What?" Stacia squeaked.

"Angel and Veronica will both be here to run the store tomorrow. I'll handle the workshop while y'all make the trip."

"I can stay here and work," Ross offered, as uncomfortable with the road trip idea as Stacia obviously was.

"Y'all tiptoe around each other like an earthworm circling a prickly pear cactus. Best icebreaker I know is a road trip. And besides, Stacia will need muscle to help load the bathtubs."

"Shouldn't we work on what we have before we bring more in?" she reasoned.

"We've got plenty of room in the warehouse and running out of material will slow us down more than y'all taking a day. Besides, the dealers might deal with somebody else if we don't jump on it. And if you wait until the weekend, you won't have the delivery truck at your disposal."

"I guess you're right." Her tone sounded as if she were facing the firing squad. "I'll get the twins ready in the morning and get them off to school while you help Daddy feed. We'll leave when I get back."

"Sounds like a plan." Ross tightened a screw. The road trip would shake things up a bit. But she looked like she might lose her lunch at the thought.

"I'll get the kids ready for church tonight." Maverick looked past Ross to Stacia. "Supper before or after?"

"After. I'll give them a snack when they get home."

"Should be any minute." Maverick checked his watch. "Coming to church with us tonight, Ross?"

"I'd like to."

"Anytime. At least there, y'all are on the same wavelength." The older man headed back to the store. "Better get back to work."

"Do you go on scavenging trips often?"

"Most of our stuff comes from Daddy's salvage business. But from time to time, I hit other stores."

"Sounds fun."

"It can be."

He could almost hear her unspoken thoughts, *if you weren't coming.*

* * *

Ross followed Maverick to the livestock barn the next morning.

He had gone to Wednesday night Bible study with them last night. They were good people, well respected in the community and they genuinely loved his niece and nephew. There was no easy fix here.

How could he let his parents in on Mason and Madison's existence while they continued to live here in Medina? His folks wouldn't be content with long-distance grandparenting after missing out on the first five years of the twins' lives. If only Houston was closer.

Temperatures had dipped to the mid-sixties during the night. But the sun was already hard at work, burning off the dew.

Ross knew the drill without thinking. He and Maverick tag teamed opening feed sacks, pouring grain into the long troughs.

Finished with their task, Maverick took the head while Ross took the heel, walking the seemingly endless line of cattle, counting each as they went.

At the end, they faced each other as a trickle of sweat tickled a trail between Ross's shoulder blades.

"One hundred twenty-three cows and eighteen calves." Maverick adjusted his hat.

"Same here."

"A mighty fine day for everyone to behave."

Ross was torn with dreading the road trip and being relieved all of the cattle were accounted for. If any of the livestock hadn't shown up, he'd have spent the day riding out to find them and possibly repairing fences, which could turn into an all-day problem. Avoiding Stacia in the process.

On the other hand, the cattle needed to continue behaving themselves until the B and B order was complete. When had he started caring about the ranch and the store? He was here for the twins and he'd met Maverick and Stacia only six days ago. But since then he'd been with one or both of them most of his waking hours, and their concerns had become his.

"Let's put out some fresh hay bales."

The two men hoisted rectangular blocks of hay out of the barn and Ross went to work cutting the twine. The first few days, he'd tried to do all the heavy lifting and let Maverick worry about strings. But the older man obviously liked carrying his own weight. Every once in a while at the end of the day, he had a slight limp—the knee trouble Stacia had mentioned—but overall Maverick was as strong and capable as a man half his age.

"Stacia's been through a lot." Finished with the bales, Maverick leaned on the rail fence, facing Ross. Pain dwelled in the depths of his blue eyes.

"I'm sorry for your loss. A wife and a daughter—you're a strong man."

"She doesn't need to lose anyone else. Neither do I."

"I'll do my best to come up with a compromise where no one gets hurt. Especially the kids."

If Mom and Dad could visit back and forth often, everything would be so much easier. But they were four hours away with a thriving business that consumed their time. Once he told them about the twins, his parents would want to spend time with them.

Maverick shook his head. "I don't see how you can do that. But I'll hold you to it."

"Fair enough." Surely his parents wouldn't want to uproot the twins. How had he become caught in the middle, between his family and people he barely knew? His brother's hijinks had caused all his troubles, as usual. He should be used to it by now.

"Y'all better git." The older man checked his watch. "And I better git to the workshop."

"Are you sure I should go with her? I could stay here and work."

"Nah. She doesn't want you to go. But she'd have a hissy fit if I let you stay here alone with the kids."

"Do you think she'll ever trust me with them?"

"Besides her mama and sister dying on her, she's had other folks let her down. You'll have to spend a lot of hours showing her you can be trusted."

Other folks, such as the creepy, selfish principal.

"I trust you'll be extra careful with her heart." Maverick's gaze narrowed. "It's tender emotionally. And physically."

What was he getting at? "I'm not looking to date your daughter, if that's what you mean. The twins are my reason for being here."

"I know that, but I also know my daughter is a lovely girl, just like her mother. Y'all are about the same age. Both unattached. And I'm not blind. I've seen you looking at her."

Ross's face heated. What could he say to that? Guilty as charged. He'd noticed her beauty. More than that, he'd seen her gentleness and obvious love for the twins. He had to tread carefully. Under different circumstances, she'd be exactly the type of woman he could fall for. But her heart had already been damaged by two painful losses.

But wait, what had Maverick said? Her heart had been damaged emotionally and physically? Did she have the same condition as her mom and sister?

"Does Stacia have a heart problem?"

"I've already said too much."

If Stacia had a heart condition, could the stress of the situation with him and the twins cause her health issues? He didn't have any experience with such things.

She worked hard physically in the workshop. Most days, she broke a good sweat, sanding claw-foot tubs. And he'd seen her put her back into it to pry nails out of coffee bar parts. Surely if her health was so fragile, she'd let him do the hard stuff. And Maverick wouldn't send her on a road trip with her biggest stressor if her heart was in danger. Would he?

"Just tread carefully with her, will you?"

"You have my word." But there was the principal she might be still pining for. Didn't Maverick know she was still hung up on him?

"Good." Maverick offered his hand.

Ross clasped it, gave a firm shake.

The older man ambled toward the workshop and Ross followed, deep in thought.

His gut twisted. Just in case her heart was weak, he couldn't afford to upset her.

The way he saw it, he had two options. Figure out a compromise where the twins stayed put but his folks visited often, which would be difficult because of his parents' business and the distance between them. Or find out if she still wanted the principal enough to share the kids with his folks.

The fifteen-minute trip to Bandera had passed in silence. They'd gotten enough pieces and parts for fifteen coffee bars, along with fifty claw-foot tubs, and gotten a good deal on all of them.

But then she'd gotten stuck in Daddy's truck with her worst nightmare for the hour drive to Fredericksburg. Yet in many ways, she liked Ross. He was great with the twins and he'd taken a large load off her shoulders with the B and B order. On top of being a hard worker, he was kind and genuinely wanted to attend church.

"It's right here." She pulled into the flea market's lot and parked. As soon as she killed the engine, she was out.

They entered the dimly lit ancient building. The scent of old books, dust and that antique dresser drawer smell that was so hard to conquer greeted them.

A familiar gray-haired lady sat behind the counter.

"Hi, Maisy."

"Stacia, so good to see you again. Oh my, I didn't know you had a fella. And a might handsome one at that."

Her face steamed. "This is Ross. Our new hire at the store. That's all." Except he was the twins' uncle and they had to work something out without ripping her niece and nephew in half.

"Oh, my mistake. I believe the coffee bar pieces you might be interested in are in booths eleven and thirty-six. There are two claw foots in twenty-two and there's an old table in the back I'll show you. Then we'll head to the warehouse, where all the really good stuff is." Maisy rubbed her hands together as if she couldn't wait. "Follow me."

It always amazed Stacia the pace Maisy kept. In her late sixties to early seventies, she was terribly humped from osteoporosis. But that didn't stop her from flitting about quickly.

"I know you said you're building the table part of the coffee bar, but I thought this might save you some time." Maisy unlocked the dust-coated door in the back marked Employees Only and waved them through. "I could let you have it for twenty bucks."

Stacia's eyes widened at the small Queen Anne–style entry table.

"No!" Ross shouted. "That's a Chippendale."

"He's right," Stacia agreed. "It's easily worth fifteen hundred."

"It is?" Maisy wrung her hands. "This little thing? Well, I said I'd let you have it for twenty and I'm not a deal breaker."

"Oh Maisy, I couldn't possibly keep you to that deal. I want you to clean this table up. Don't sand it or anything, but polish it and put it on the floor for what it's worth."

"I'm such a failure at this." Maisy pressed her hand to her temple. "My Alford knew what things were, how much they were worth. I should sell the store and be done with it."

"You're not a failure, Maise. You're learning."

"I should have paid more attention when he was alive."

"Do you enjoy running the store, Maisy?" Ross asked.

"I do. Very much. I feel so close to Alford here." She clasped a hand to her heart. "He loved this place. I just don't know what I'm doing is all."

"I have an idea." He fished something out of his pocket, then handed Maisy a business card. "I'm an appraiser. When you get a new piece in, you text me or email me a picture. I'll tell you where the markings will be if it's a real antique and quote the value. When you sell it, you send me ten percent of what you sold it for."

"You'd do that?"

"I won't let anyone take advantage of you, Maisy. It's just not right."

"I'll do that." Maisy threw her arms around him. "Oh, thank you, young man. You've made an old woman very happy."

"I'm glad to help." Ross grinned as he hugged her back.

Stacia blinked tears away. She'd worried about people taking Maisy for a ride since Alford's death. But she'd been at a loss how to help except on her infrequent visits to Maisy's store.

"Here." Maisy finally let go of him. "Let me show you the rest of the stuff."

They spent the next hour picking and bargaining a fair price. In the end, they got enough doors and parts for another thirty-four coffee bars along with twenty-three claw-foot tubs. She wrote Maisy a nice check with plenty of room for profit from Waverly's B and B's.

Thirty minutes later, they were loaded and back on the road headed to the ranch. The air conditioning swept a chill over Stacia's heated skin. She'd probably sweated off all her makeup while helping Ross load the truck.

"That was really nice of you to help Maisy out. I'm guessing you usually get paid more than that."

"I usually charge by the hour. But I figure she's struggling and there's no telling what shysters have carried out of her store for little or nothing. She's due for a break."

"She's a sweetheart."

"Speaking of sweethearts, tell me more about Adrian Caruthers."

She frowned, didn't take her eyes off the road. "What about him?"

"He still has a thing for you."

"He broke up with me."

"Because of the twins."

"Sort of."

"What if you didn't have them through the week? If you only had them on weekends, do you think y'all could work things out?"

"But I have them. All of the time." Her tone turned ominous. "And who said I wanted to work things out with him?"

"You didn't have to. You showed me."

"Oh really?" Her right eyebrow went up. "When was that?"

"You got teary over him in the drop-off line the other day."

"For your information," she snapped, "I didn't get teary over him."

"Okay, just calm down." Now that he knew about her heart, he needed to remember not to upset her.

"Don't tell me to calm down."

"Then at least pull over."

She huffed out a big breath and pulled into a grocery store lot. "I was never hung up on Adrian. He was into me way more than I was him. I was about to break it off when Calli died and everything went crazy."

"So why the tears?"

"If you must know," her hair seemed to get redder with her temper, "I have the same heart defect as my mother and sister. They both died because childbirth put a strain on their hearts." Her voice cracked as she turned to face him. "Doctors have recommended that I never have children."

"Oh Stacia." And it was obvious how much she loved the twins. That she'd dreamed of having her own kids someday. With her heart defect, he should have figured it out. "I'm so sorry. I had no clue."

"You definitely have no clue." Her chin quivered. "If you think you can do me a favor and take the twins off my hands so I can have my happily-ever-after, you've got another thing coming. They *are* my happily-ever-after. I won't let you take them." She punctuated each word with a jab of her finger. "Do you hear me?"

"I hear you. Just calm down. We'll work something out."

"I won't have a heart attack just because I'm upset.

Okay? It's not like I'm a ticking time bomb. It takes more strain than you to kill me off." She rolled her eyes. "But then you're probably hoping I'll keel over, so you can have Mason and Madison."

"No, Stacia, you're wrong. That's not what I want. The twins love you. They need you."

"You got that right."

"Why don't you let me drive."

She turned away, sat there staring at the wheel. "I'm okay, just give me a minute."

"I'm sorry I upset you."

"What makes you think I'm upset? Because my face is all splotchy? Welcome to redhead world." Another deep breath seeped out of her and she turned back onto the highway.

The rest of the drive home was silent.

Chapter Five

If only it weren't Friday. Stacia sanded the final rust spot on the tub. Weekends were always busiest at the store, which meant that even though Angel and Veronica were both working, Daddy was in the store all day. Leaving her alone in the workshop with Ross. Making the afternoon drag on. She'd asked Daddy to take the kids to school this morning to avoid Adrian. Torn between dodging two men.

Somehow Ross knowing her truth made her dread working with him less than seeing the school principal. Maybe his harsh words toward Adrian had stirred up her anger again. Even though she'd planned to break things off with him, when Adrian had rejected Mason and Madison, it had infuriated her. She needed to pray about it and get rid of the bitterness toward him.

In the meantime, she'd kept her back to Ross and her drill on most of the day as she smoothed one claw-foot bathtub after another, effectively killing any chance for chitchat. The mere memory of their conversation yesterday still heated her skin.

Anger smoldered within her, but so did embarrassment. For letting him see her so upset, for letting him in on her secret. Only Daddy had known she shouldn't have children. Until now.

The rust disintegrated and she set down her drill, turned to check the corbels and hooks heating in the crockpot.

Ross stood there, peering into it. "I hope that's not supper."

"Heating them in a crockpot takes the old layers of paint right off." She grabbed a set of tongs, fished the finished pieces out and laid them on a towel.

"About yesterday."

"Can we just not go there?" She closed her eyes.

"Just hear me out and we won't go there again. I'm really sorry. Really. I didn't mean to insult you. I've just been racking my brain trying to figure out a way where everyone can be happy."

He massaged his temples, as if warding off a headache. "I didn't mean I'd take the twins and you'd never see them. I meant we'd share them. If you'd wanted that, we'd have worked out a schedule of equal time with them. But you don't want that. I'm done with that idea and back to the drawing board."

"Good."

"Good. I just can't stop thinking about Adrian."

"Why?" She frowned.

"It takes a selfish, special kind of jerk to break up with a woman he's obviously interested in because she can't have kids and live. I mean we're talking life and death here."

"Actually." She drew in a deep breath. "I never told him. When I got the twins and he said he wanted to raise his own kids, not someone else's, I took it to mean he wouldn't be interested in me if he knew the truth." She blinked away tears. "I'm done with this subject."

"I am too. I just want you to know that you'll find the

right man one day. And helping you raise the twins and not having any children of his own won't matter to him. A man would be blessed to marry you."

His kind words lodged a lump in her throat.

"Thanks." She swallowed hard, then slipped a mask over her mouth and nose, and handed him one. "I'll be painting."

"Is this what you had in mind?" He gestured toward the coffee bar he'd been working on.

Searching for flaws, she inspected the piece, but there weren't any. The six-panel door joined seamlessly to the small table he'd built with the plywood top with perfectly beveled edges and spindle legs. The corbels at the top held a sturdy shelf and eight antique cast iron hooks lined the space between the shelf and tabletop. He'd painted it all white with each door panel contrasting in yellow. Exactly the way she'd imagined it.

"It's perfect." Ross had proven to be invaluable this week in the workshop, bringing to life the images in her head, and keeping them ahead of their quota to meet their B and B deadline. If only he wasn't Mason and Madison's uncle.

The twins loved him and he obviously was crazy about them already. With his clueless parents lurking, how could they possibly come to a compromise that would give everyone involved time with the kids, without turning their world upside down?

The door from the store opened and Mason ran in. "Aunt Stacia, Uncle Ross, we're home."

"For a whole weekend." Madison followed, and shut the door behind her. "Can we do something fun?"

"Like what?" Stacia set her paint gun down. Though her mind had been on the twins, she hadn't realized it was time for them to come home from school yet.

"Ride horses or go for a hike or a picnic or go to the park in Bandera."

She pulled her mask off over her head. "What about homework?"

"We don't got any," Mason said.

"We don't *have* any," she corrected.

"That's what I said." Mason frowned.

"You said *got*. *Have* is proper English." Stacia pulled her smock off, hung it on a hook. "*Don't* and *got* never go together. It's always *don't have*. How about a horseback ride, since that was first on the list?"

"Yay." Madison clapped her hands.

"Come on, Uncle Ross, come with us."

"He can't." She quickly cut off the possibility. "He has to stay here and paint the bathtub I was about to do and he has more coffee bars to build."

"Your aunt's right." Ross shot the twins a wink. "But I tell you what—I'll work extra late tonight and get us good and ahead on our order, so I can hang with y'all tomorrow. How's that sound?"

"Awesome." Mason held his hand up for a high five and Ross smacked it.

Dreadful. If Ross played with the twins tomorrow, she'd be tempted to stay busy in the workshop. Even though she'd rather be with her niece and nephew.

Why did he have to be here? Everything had been great. Until he'd shown up.

It had been well after midnight when Ross left the workshop last night. He'd had supper with the twins, Maverick and a stiff Stacia. Once the kids had gone to bed he and Maverick had gone back to work. The older man had left around ten thirty.

Ross stretched the aching muscles in his back, wishing he'd left that early, then knocked on the door of the Keyes' farmhouse. But the extra work was worth getting to spend part of his Saturday with Mason and Madison. The more time he spent with them, the more they wound themselves around his heart and the guiltier he felt for not telling his folks.

But before he broke the news to his parents, he wanted to have a solution. A solution that hadn't come to him just yet.

The door opened and Stacia stood there, looking bright and sunny in a yellow button-up blouse paired with jeans and boots.

"What's on the agenda. Another horseback ride?"

"No."

"Good to see you too."

"I mean, the twins want to go to a dude ranch in Bandera. They have outdoor bowling, putt-putt golf and an indoor water park and swimming pool."

"Sounds fun. I'll get a few things and meet you at your car."

"Sure." She sounded even less excited than she looked.

He hurried back to his apartment, grabbed a pair of cutoff jeans and a towel. By the time he got back to the farmhouse, she was herding the twins into the car. Had she planned on leaving without him?

"Uncle Ross!" Mason darted toward him.

"In the car," Stacia ordered.

"But Uncle Ross is here."

"You better do what your aunt says, kiddo. Because I'm coming with you."

"You are?" Mason's eyes grew wide.

"And the last one in the car is a rotten cow patty."

"Ewww!" Mason bolted for the car.

Ross followed, caught Stacia's eye. "You weren't trying to get gone before I got back, now were you?"

"Of course not. I've come to realize you're not that easy to get rid of," she mumbled. "It just takes forever to get these two in sync."

He eased his long legs into the passenger side. "We can take my truck any time, you know."

"That would give you entirely too much control and besides, I still don't know if you're a good driver."

"How can we find out if Uncle Ross is a good driver, if you never let him drive?" Madison asked.

"Hmm. You've got a good point there." Stacia made eye contact with the twins in the rearview mirror. "Maybe we can follow him to church tomorrow."

A worthy adversary. She'd just kicked him out of riding with them in the morning.

They'd made strides at getting along, at her trusting him. Until he'd tried the whole Adrian angle. He could kick himself. Not the way to win her trust at all.

"Two kids—check, ten towels—four for each sopping twin and one for each adult—check, dry clothes for two kids—check, dry clothes for me—check, sunblock—check. I think we've got everything."

Along with an unwanted cowboy, he could almost hear her thinking it.

"Do you have towels and extra clothes, Uncle Ross?" Madison asked.

"I do."

"Then let's go already." Mason bounced in his car seat.

The fifteen-minute drive to Bandera was filled with the twins' chatter about what all they wanted to do once they got to the dude ranch. From the sound of it, they'd have to stay a whole week to get it all done.

"Here we are." Stacia turned into a drive with a petting

zoo along the side filled with sheep, ponies and rabbits. A chapel sat off to the other side with a large barn-looking structure on down the drive.

As she parked beside the barn, he caught a glimpse of the putt-putt course—dotted with barrels, wagon wheels and enormous cowboy boots.

"What do y'all want to do first?"

"Swim." Both young voices blended.

"They always want to swim first." Stacia chuckled. "And then they're cold while we play putt-putt because their hair is wet. But it's supposed to be eighty-eight today, so maybe that will help."

"Aunt Stacia always wants to play putt-putt." Madison unbuckled her seatbelt. "But she's terrible at it."

"Hey." Stacia's tone dripped with insult. "You don't have to win to have fun."

"Well that's good. Cuz you'll never win, Aunt Stacia." Mason was already loose and trying to open the door, but apparently Stacia had the child locks engaged in the back of the car.

"Hold up, partner." Ross climbed out, heard a click, then helped Mason out, but held on to the child's hand.

"Let's go." Mason tugged toward the barn structure.

"Slow down, Mase. We've got all afternoon," Stacia cautioned as she helped Madison out of the car, then opened the hatch and pulled out a large drawstring bag stuffed to the brim with something.

"He's always in a hurry." Madison rolled her eyes. But Stacia must not have seen since there was no admonishment.

"I guess the pool is in the barn?" Ross took the bag. Felt like towels.

"It is." Stacia rounded the car holding Madison's hand. "They have an outdoor pool on the other side of the putt-

putt course and I think it's still open, but all three of us burn easy, so we usually stick with the indoor facilities for swimming since we're in the sun during mini golf."

He matched her stride, probably making them look like a family. If only they could be. If only his folks lived right down the street and they could all visit whenever they liked, sharing the twins without disrupting their lives.

As they reached the barn, glass doors offered a glimpse of a pool with lots of slides and chutes on one end. Inside, a teenage girl stood in a booth near a turnstile entry.

"Let me get this." Ross fished his wallet out of his back pocket.

"You don't have to do that." Stacia dug around in her huge beach bag–style purse. "Two adults, two kids. All day please."

The girl quoted a price.

"I want to." He slipped the bills through the window.

"Thank you." The girl smiled. "Once you change, you can come back here to put your things in a locker if you like."

"Thanks."

They entered through the turnstile one at a time.

Stacia dug in her purse, then doled out the twins' swimsuits. "Now go change, but no running." Her tone turned stern. "Remember last time you ran, Mason, and the lifeguard made you sit in the corner."

"Yes ma'am."

"Everyone else is already here." Madison scanned the pool.

Stacia waved at someone. "We'll wait right here until you're both changed."

The kids scurried into dressing rooms with individual doors and Ross followed the direction of her gaze. Two couples. He'd seen them all at church. The women had huddled up with Stacia at church Sunday and Wednesday. And he'd gotten the distinct impression they'd been talking about him. Maybe from the furtive glances cast his way.

"Remind me what your friends' names are. I remember Jayda and her folks, but I can't come up with their names."

"Larae and Rance Shepherd. Her mom and mine were friends, so we've been friends forever. The brunette is Lexie Parker and that's Clint Rawlins, her fiancé. Lexie's folks work at Larae's ranch, so Lexie and I became friends through Larae." Her attention turned to the pool. "With Jayda, the biggest boy in the kiddy pool is Cooper and the little girl with him is Charlee. They're Clint's nephew and niece."

He'd never get all the names straight. "Did you know they were coming?"

"Since Veronica reworked her schedule so she can be in the store on Saturdays until we get the B and B order finished, I called them last night. Even though Jayda's a couple of years older, Cooper is about the same age as the twins, and I think Charlee is three, but they all play well together."

Ross took a minute to scope out the place.

Kids flew down the slides and chutes landing in giggling splashes. On the other end of the pool, there was plenty of room for swimming, along with a small kiddy pool and a second large pool for adults. A few swam, but most sat in lawn chairs circling the kids' end, either watching their children or reading. Four lifeguards were stationed high on their perches, two per pool at each end, totally focused on their jobs.

"This place is really something."

"Until a few years ago, only guests at the dude ranch could get in. But the owners opened the activities to the public and expanded since. The indoor pool is new, along with outdoor bowling and putt-putt."

"And you like putt-putt."

"I stink at it, but it's fun. The twins get bored with it before we get through the whole course."

"Maybe we could come sometime without the kids."

The dreamy look on her face said she was tempted. But then she frowned. "I don't have time and besides I like spending my time outside of work with the twins."

Minutes later, the twins exited the changing rooms. Mason started to run, but obviously remembered her orders and slowed his pace. Both handed Stacia their clothes.

"Thank you." She folded the clothes, slipped them in her bag.

"Can we go in now?" Mason begged.

A sudden panic filled Ross's chest. "Don't y'all need life vests or something?"

"We know how to swim," Madison assured him. "Aunt Stacia got us lessons here when we were three."

"In that case, I can watch them while you change, then we'll swap," Ross suggested.

"You go ahead. I'm not planning to swim."

"Why not?"

"Don't worry about it. Go change."

"You have to come swim with us, Aunt Stacia." Mason tugged on her hand.

"Did you bring your suit?"

"Yes."

"But you're not planning to swim." He peered at her. "Let me guess. You think I might abscond with the children while you're in the dressing room."

"What does *abscond* mean?" Madison looked from Ross to Stacia.

"Come swim with us, Aunt Stacia." Mason tugged toward the changing rooms. "Please."

"Three against one." Ross raised one eyebrow at her. "The twins can get in and I promise I'll be right here watching them when you get back."

"Please, Aunt Stacia, please," both kids pleaded in unison.

"I promise." He tried to muster up all the sincerity he could.

She scrutinized him, her gaze narrowing to a warning slit, then glanced at the twins and back at him. "Right here."

"You have my word."

"Y'all can get in. But be careful and watch for other swimmers and sliders."

"Yay." The twins headed to the pool and Ross turned to watch them.

"I'll be right back." She watched until both kids were safely in the water, then glanced at both lifeguards. "And you better be here."

"I will."

She scurried over to her friends and spoke. Probably something like, "If that guy tries to leave with the twins, nab him." Then she hurried toward the dressing rooms. If she wasn't careful, the lifeguard would put her in the corner for running.

He focused solely on the twins, intent on nothing happening during his watch. Maybe Stacia would trust him if he nailed this task.

Even though she'd enlisted Rance and Clint's help in watching the kids, Stacia changed into her one-piece as fast as she could and didn't even take the time to fold her clothes. In a wad, she stashed them in the bag, opened the door and scanned the pool. Mason and Madison were climbing a ladder to one of the tube slides and Ross was right where she'd left him.

What would she have done if they'd been gone? Her heart sank to her stomach. She still didn't trust Ross, but with Rance and Clint on notice, he wouldn't have gotten far.

Even though her suit was modest, she always felt strange wearing it in public. She wrapped a towel around herself, tucked it in under her arm and headed toward him. Though she was slim, she always felt self-conscious since getting a sunburn that never turned into a tan was her best event. It simply peeled away leaving permanently milky white skin with more freckles. Thankfully, with the indoor pool, she wouldn't have to worry about sunblock until they went outside later.

"Your turn."

"That was fast." He pointed a finger at her. "You have trust issues."

"Only where you're concerned." But in truth, she trusted few. She focused on the kids, ignored him until he sauntered away.

Madison slid down the slide, screaming all the way and ending with giggles when she entered the pool with a splash.

"Come on in, Aunt Stacia," Mason hollered, as he entered the tube.

She waited until he came out the other end and surfaced. "I'm waiting for your uncle, so I can put all our stuff in a locker."

"At your service." Ross strolled up beside her. "Want me to get the locker?"

Blue jean cutoffs. No shirt with his clothes rolled in a bundle under one arm. Muscled arms and chest. Not from the gym, but hard work. What would it feel like to be safe in those arms?

"Stacia?"

"Hmm?"

"The locker."

"I'll do it since I've done it before. You have to fill out a form."

"And you don't think I can handle that?"

"Just go on in. I'll be back in a minute." She forced her gaze to stay on his as he handed over his clothing, boots, keys and wallet. Tried to ignore the tingle caused by his hand grazing her arm, as she headed for the booth. By the time she filled out a form and stashed all their possessions except for their towels, her heart was still hammering.

Ross was in the water up to his shoulders on one side of the tube slide. Since the pool was only four feet deep, he must be squatting or on his knees. At least, she couldn't see the rest of him. What was wrong with her getting so distracted by him?

"Come on in, Aunt Stacia," Madison squealed as she slid down again.

Stacia walked over to the side, slipped off her towel, sat down and dipped her toes in the water. Not too hot, not too cold as usual. She slid into the pool with a relaxed sigh.

"Watch me slide!" Mason disappeared into the tube. Seconds later, he popped out the other end with a splash. "Did you see?"

"I did."

"You have to come closer." He was always convinced she couldn't watch unless she stood near the end.

She knee-walked over to the side of the slide opposite Ross with the water swirling around her neck.

"Do they ever do anything other than slide?"

"Eventually. Sometimes we play Marco Polo if it's not

too crowded." There were only six other kids at the moment. Jayda and Cooper took turns with the twins on the tube slide since Lexie had taken over Charlee duty in the kiddy pool. Two older kids took turns on the bigger slide next to them, and two boys tossed a ball back and forth in the swimming end.

"Is it always this peaceful?"

"Depends on the time of day. Usually this early, it's not crowded. More people come after lunch and in the summer, most people go to the outdoor pool."

A huge splash sounded behind them and they both turned.

Water cascaded their faces as a boy surfaced after an obvious cannonball.

"Is it just me, or is he too old for the big kid pool?"

"Maybe he's really big for his age?" Along with rambunctious—and no parents seemed to be watching him. "It's hard to say. But if he gets out of hand, the lifeguards will take care of it. They're really good about keeping things safe here."

"Still, we better keep an eye out. Brutus could hurt someone."

She chuckled at the nickname. But the big kid was living up to it as he grabbed the smaller kids' ball and turned it into a game of keep away against their will.

The lifeguard blew a whistle. "Give them their ball back, Jimmy." His voice came through a megaphone.

The twins and their friends slid several more times, but then Brutus joined them, causing more wait time in between slides, especially since he ran in front of the smaller children and ended up with more turns.

Another whistle blew. "Jimmy, no pushing other kids aside. Wait your turn. One more infraction and you're out."

"Let's play Marco Polo." Mason swam for the other end of the pool. "Come on Cooper."

"Okay. Come on, Uncle Ross, you can play too." Madison followed, her strokes smoother than her brother's. "Come on Jayda."

Stacia stood and started after them, glad to escape Jimmy.

"Jimmy wait! Watch out, miss!" A whistle blew the alarm.

Something slammed into her back just above her waist. She pitched forward, tried to scream. But nothing came out. She couldn't breathe.

Strong arms came around her, kept her from going under. "I've got you." Ross pressed her face into his chest. "Kids, get out of the pool, and stay where I can see you."

"Aunt Stacia!" Madison screamed.

Panic squeezed her empty lungs.

"She'll be okay." Ross sounded so calm.

"I've got Madison and Mason," Larae called. "Don't worry."

"Relax," Ross murmured near her ear. "Just got the wind knocked out of you. Try to take some deep breaths."

Blessed oxygen returned as her breathing stabilized. But now that her chest didn't hurt, her back sure did.

"Ma'am, are you all right?" The lifeguard had entered the pool, not the young college-aged girl, but a man.

"I think so." She pressed her hand against her back. Madison and Mason sat on the side of the pool, their faces panic-stricken.

"I'm so sorry, ma'am. I thought he'd wait until you got past thc slide."

"I'll be fine. I shouldn't have walked in front of it."

"We've had trouble with Jimmy all week, which is why I took on lifeguard duty. His parents are staying at the ranch and they send him down here by himself. He's twelve, but he's so big, and he won't follow the rules." Irritation edged the lifeguard's tone. "But he's out now. He can't come back unless his parents come with him."

"Maybe we should go to the doctor, get checked out," Ross suggested.

"The ranch will pay for any doctor bills you incur. Just have them send me the bill." The lifeguard offered his hand. "Chase Donovan, owner."

"I don't think that's necessary. I think I'll just be sore for a few days."

"I'm really sorry this happened."

"It's not your fault."

"I should have kicked Jimmy out before now. But I feel sorry for him. He craves attention and his parents don't seem to give him any."

"That's sad."

"Poor kid." Ross frowned.

"I've seen thousands like him here over the years." Mr. Donovan sighed. "I'm just sorry you got caught in the crosshairs. I'm serious about the doctor. Go get checked out and give them the dude ranch number for the bill."

"I'm sure I'll be fine. I'm just glad it was me and not one of the smaller kids."

"It could have been much worse. Well at least take advantage of the hot tub. Works wonders on sore muscles." Mr. Donovan scanned the swimmers lingering around the pool or with their parents. "I better get back to work." He blew his whistle. "Y'all can get back in the pool now. All except Jimmy, you come with me."

The boy stood off to the side with one of the male lifeguards. He fell in step behind Mr. Donovan but mocked the way the owner walked. Obviously still not taking the situation seriously.

She'd always wanted to relax in the spa, but she was always too busy on twin patrol. Standing at the side of the pool with Larae, Madison and Mason were calm now that they'd seen she was okay. Patiently waiting. Even though they had the owner's okay to get back in the water, they were waiting for her.

The round swell of Larae's nine-month pregnancy lodged a twinge in her chest. Something she'd never have.

"Here's an idea." Ross gripped her shoulders, turned her toward the large round tub full of bubbling water. "You go relax, I've got twin duty."

"But—"

"You can watch to make sure I don't abscond with Mason and Madison. And besides, you've got your posse over there watching me."

Oh so tempting. Especially since the spa was empty at the moment. She wasn't the communal hot tub type, unless she knew the other people in it.

"Okay, here are your choices—go sit in the spa while I swim with the kids, or I'm taking you to the doctor."

"I'm not going to the doctor."

"Then get in the spa."

She propped her hands on her hips. "You're not the boss of me."

"No. But I am bigger than you." A sly grin settled on his lips.

"So you're gonna bully me?" She pinned him with a narrowed gaze.

"If that's what it takes. Want me to carry you to the spa?"

"You okay, Stace?" Rance asked.

"Fine. Just lost my wind there for a minute."

Murmurs from the other parents caught her attention. She wouldn't put it past Ross to make a spectacle.

"All right, I'm going." She walked over to the twins. "I'm okay."

"That was so scary." Madison shuddered.

"Yes, it was. New rule, if a kid like that gets in the pool, we get out, okay?"

"Okay," the twins echoed.

"But do we have to leave now?" Mason asked.

"No. I'll go soak in the hot tub, so maybe I won't be sore in the morning. Uncle Ross will stay in the pool with y'all."

"Yay." Mason clapped his hands.

She climbed the steps out of the pool, retrieved her towel and wrapped up in it, then padded over to the hot tub. As she stepped down into the warm water and shed her towel, goose bumps swept over her. Her neck and shoulders were a bit achy, similar to whiplash. She settled into the bubbling foam, with a pulsing jet between her shoulder blades and one on her back at the point of impact.

What would have happened if Ross hadn't been there? She'd have gone under for certain. Unable to breathe, would she have taken on water? With the twins still in the water, Larae would have seen to them and the owner would have come to her aid. But she and the twins would have been in a worse panic. And once she got her breath back, she probably would have wanted to leave, cutting the twins' fun Saturday short.

Instead, they were fine, back to taking turns sliding down the tube with their friends.

"Come on, Uncle Ross, slide with us."

"I don't know if I can fit."

"Sure you can in the big one." Mason laughed. "I dare you."

"Well in that case…" With an impish grin shot in her direction, Ross climbed the ladder of the largest slide. At the top of the tube, he stood, peering down to make sure all the kids were out of the way. "Look out below." He disappeared in the tube, then popped out the other end and landed in the water with a major splash.

To the giggling delight of both happy twins.

She never would have imagined it could happen, but for once as the pulsing water eased her aches, she was glad Ross was here.

"You okay?" Lexie asked.

Stacia opened her eyes to see her friend descend into the hot tub.

"I'm fine. Are the twins okay?"

"They're fine. Rance and Clint are in the pool with them on kid patrol. And Ross watch."

"You'll be stove-up tomorrow." Larae settled in a lounge chair beside the spa. "I'm with Mr. Donovan, you should see a doctor."

"I'm sure it's just bruising."

"You should come by our ranch every day and soak in our unused hot tub. It's just languishing on the back porch, since the doctor deemed it off limits for me until after the baby." A hint of longing threaded through Larae's voice. "We can visit until you feel better."

"Maybe."

"We want to hear all about things with Ross." Lexie perched diagonally across from her.

"Shh, he's right over there."

"There's no way he can hear." Larae peered at her. "But just relax for now. We'll get it out of you sooner or later."

And she knew they would. Even if they had to physically drag her to Larae's ranch.

Chapter Six

After Stacia's accident yesterday, they'd ended up not playing putt-putt after all. Despite her protests, Ross had driven her straight to a clinic when they'd left, but the doctor had found only bruising. How sore would she be today? Would she end up missing church?

He climbed the farmhouse porch steps and rang the bell. Minutes passed before it swung open. Stacia stood in the threshold. Her flowing purple dress skimmed her curves and hit just above her knees. Still barefoot.

"How are you feeling?"

She grimaced. "Like an overgrown twelve-year-old drop-kicked me with both feet."

He winced. "You going to church?"

"Yes. And you're driving your own rig. Remember, we're following so I can check out your driving."

Anything to keep from riding with him. "Do I have to remind you that I drove you home yesterday?"

"No. But I was in pain, so I couldn't tell you how you drove."

"I got us home safely though."

"Oh, all right. The only vehicle we can all fit in is my SUV."

"Actually, my truck is four-door. I can fit three comfortably in the back seat. And I bought car seats for Mason and Madison." He held his hands up as if to ward off a blow. "Not to do any absconding. Just so you won't have to drive all the time and to keep from swapping safety seats back and forth."

"Like I said, we'll see." She stepped aside. "Come on in. Daddy's wrangling the kids."

He followed her into the family room, where she gingerly eased into a wingback chair.

"Are you sure you're okay?"

"Just sore. The doctor's X-ray didn't show anything amiss."

"Might slow you down in the workshop this week."

"I can't afford that."

"I can take up your slack. Once we got back yesterday, I hit the workshop, got two more claw foots done." Despite worrying about her.

She seemed surprised. "After working there late Friday night?" Sincerity softened her eyes. "Thank you. For the tubs. And for yesterday."

"I'll do whatever it takes to ensure you get the B and B order completed on time."

"No. I mean, I appreciate that." She paused, grimaced while slipping on her heels, as if simply lifting each foot hurt. "More than you can imagine. But I meant the pool incident. Thank you for being there. For helping to ease my panic. And making sure the kids stayed safe until I got my wits about me. I don't know what I'd have done if you hadn't been there."

"Not a problem. I love them too."

"I can tell." She sized him up. "I've just had them for so long. I mean Daddy helps, but the bulk of the responsibility for raising them and making sure they're healthy and happy has been mostly on me." She closed her eyes. "I have to admit, it's been nice to have someone to take up the slack. I've wanted to get in that hot tub for years."

"Are you saying you're glad to have me here?"

"In that instant of chaos—yes." She pursed her lips. "But don't get used to it."

He'd thought they'd made headway. "You can trust me, Stacia. Yesterday should have proven it. I could have left you to the lifeguards and fled with the kids, called my folks, and disappeared with them. But I didn't."

That familiar current of suspicion widened her eyes. "Sounds like it crossed your mind with a plan in place."

"Come on, I came up with that scenario because it's what you expect. I have their best interest at heart, just as you do."

She blew out a big breath. "The whole situation is impossible. I'm not good at sharing them. Especially when your folks live so far away. I just don't want them constantly dragged back and forth."

"It's only four hours." He ran his hand along the fireplace mantle, one of the most exquisitely restored pieces he'd ever seen. "And I've been trying to come up with a solution. Maybe my folks could come visit every other weekend. And on holidays and in the summer, maybe I could come get them for a visit."

"It's not ideal. But I guess it's better than them going to Houston." Her voice cracked. "Permanently."

"Uncle Ross." Mason scurried down the stairs with Madison and Maverick lagging behind. "Are you going to church with us?"

"I wouldn't miss it."

"Let's load up." Maverick clapped his hands.

Ross opened the door, held it as the Keyes family members filed out. In the last week, he'd seen enough to realize the twins were happy here. Stacia and Maverick loved and nurtured them. The kids needed to stay here, the only home they'd ever known.

But he had no idea how his parents would react when they learned they'd been robbed of grandchildren. He didn't think they'd go to court in an effort to reclaim the years they'd lost. He'd do his level best to convince his folks to be content letting Madison and Mason stay with people who'd loved them from the beginning. But he couldn't make any promises.

Stacia turned into her friend's drive. At the end of a very long Monday in the workshop with Ross, she was due a break. Despite the grilling she'd get, her sore back longed for Larae's hot tub. Even though the heat of the day had hit eighty-seven.

"Can we ride the pony?" Mason leaned to the side peering between the front seats.

"I don't know. You'll have to check with Denny." Since she was banged up and hadn't been as productive as usual today, Daddy had promised to work on coffee bars and tubs with Ross for the evening, leaving her to supervise the twins alone for a change. She parked in the drive and disengaged the child safety lock on the back doors. Both doors opened and the twins bolted toward the barn.

Most of the time, she got out first so she could corral the twins. But here, it was just like home—they knew the rules about staying on this side of the fences unless they were with an adult. Gingerly, she eased herself out with the muscles in her back protesting loudly.

Denny popped out of the barn, gave her a wave to let her know the kids were supervised.

"There she is. Granny lost her get up and go." Larae walked across the porch with a bit of a waddle, wearing shorts and a tank top. As petite and lean as she'd always been, except for her belly.

"You got that right." Stacia stretched, then made her way to the house.

"You two make me feel young and spry." Lexie chuckled.

"I look and feel like I swallowed a beach ball."

"Stop it, you're the cutest pregnant woman I've ever seen." Stacia bit her lip, forced a smile. "I always figured I'd gain all over the way Calli did."

"Well she did have twins, so that might have been part of it," Lexie reasoned. "But if you're day-dreaming about babies, you might want to find a husband."

"I'm not in any rush." Conversations like this hurt the most. When she tried to keep things light, act like she was normal, that the only thing keeping her from having a family was the lack of a husband. "Are you sure your dad's okay watching the kids?"

"Jayda's with him and Rance is too. They're fine." Larae linked arms with both of them as they made their way down the side of the wraparound porch to the well-shaded hot tub in the back. "I think Ross is a prime candidate for husband material."

"No way." Stacia shook her head. "He makes my brain want to explode."

"Only because you're worried about the twins. I can tell he's fallen in love with them." Lexie gave her a gentle elbow jab. "Men who love kids make excellent husbands. Just think about it. If he was just some guy with no ties to the twins, would you be interested?"

"I can't separate the two. He's Mason and Madison's uncle. All he makes me feel is anxiety. And aren't we trying to relax here? Subject change in order. How are the wedding plans coming along?"

"Making me want to pull my hair out and elope," Lexie admitted.

"Just stick with it." Larae ushered them into the hot tub, then claimed a lawn chair. Three lemonade glasses lined the rim. "You'll be glad someday when you have the pictures and memories of having your family and friends celebrate your special day. I just hope this baby gives up the nest soon so I don't go into labor in the middle of the ceremony."

"If you elope, Larae and I will never speak to you again." Stacia eased down into the tub and the warm pulsing water went to work on the tenderness in her back. "We want to wear our pretty red dresses. Finally, someone came up with bridesmaid dresses that aren't hideous."

"Please. Y'all could never look hideous." Lexie's smile turned sappy. "I can't believe in two weeks, I'll be Mrs. Clint Rawlins."

"He's still feeling good and not having any residual issues from his bull wreck last year?" Larae asked.

"Doing great. No memory problems, all back to normal."

"I'm glad he's fully recovered." Stacia sipped her lemonade. "I'm sure it had something to do with having a great therapist named Lexie."

"We saw his neurologist last week. All his tests came back normal. The doctor said to go live his life."

"That's wonderful." Larae held her glass up. "Cheers."

They clinked their lemonade glasses.

"I worry about the bull riders at my rodeo," Larae said.

"Trust me, if you didn't own a rodeo, they'd just go somewhere else. I'm so glad Clint quit." Lexie settled lower in the tub. "He's completely content with just watching. You should bring the twins sometime, Stacia. We're there with Cooper and Charlee just about every weekend."

"It would be fun and I'd love to support Larae, but I'm terrified Mason would decide he wants to be a bull rider when he grows up." A shudder went through her despite the warm day and heated water.

"Oh!" Larae dropped her glass, clutched her stomach. Her glass bounced off her knee and landed in the bubbling water.

"You okay?" Stacia grabbed the glass before it sank, set it outside the tub.

"Just a twinge." Larae clenched her teeth.

"Looks like more than that from your expression." Lexie set her glass down. "What do you say, we get out and go inside?"

"I'm fine." Larae waved a hand as if it was nothing. "Ow!"

"I'm an occupational therapist, not a midwife. Let's go inside."

"I'm not sure I can stand." Larae moaned. "It's been a few years, but I think that was a contraction."

"When did they start?" Lexie checked her watch.

"I've had a few twinges today, but this just started."

"I'm calling Rance." Stacia grabbed her phone.

The pain seemed to subside and Lexie helped Larae stand. As they made their way toward the house, another wave hit and Larae doubled over, then crumpled to the deck.

Rance picked up. "Hello."

"Hey, it's Stacia. Can you come to the house?" She tried to sound calm.

"Is Larae all right?"

"Um, I think she might be in labor."

"Coffee bar number fifty-seven, ready for paint." Ross ran his hand over the joints, strong and sturdy.

The back door of the workshop opened and Stacia ushered Madison and Mason inside.

"I need y'all to watch the kids. Larae just went into labor, so I'm going to the hospital." She was flustered, with pink splotches mottling her cheeks and shaking hands.

"We got this." Maverick winked at the twins. "I need some help anyway."

"Are you sure you're okay to drive?" Ross asked.

"I'm fine."

"Maybe Ross should drive you."

"I don't need a driver."

"You look pretty shaky. That settles it, Ross you drive her." Maverick tweaked Mason's nose. "You can't paint with these two here anyway. Somebody won't keep a mask on. We're ahead on the order and I can finish up here."

"You heard the man." Ross took off his sleeved apron.

"Just because he says it, doesn't mean we have to do it. I can drive myself."

"We kind of do. He's my boss and your dad."

"I like the way you think, Ross." Daddy grinned.

"We know Uncle Ross is a good driver now." Madison concurred. "And Aunt Stacia is really nervous."

"Hold on and let me wash up a bit." Ross hurried to the bathroom, dipped a generous dollop of Goop cleaner on his hands and scrubbed. Most of the paint came off.

When he stepped out of the bathroom, Stacia was still there, tapping her foot in irritation. He'd half expected her to bolt.

He hurried to the door, opened it for her. "After you."

She rolled her eyes.

"You're not supposed to roll your eyes, Aunt Stacia," Madison admonished.

"You're absolutely right," Stacia admitted with a sheepish grin. "I was being a bad example and I'm sorry."

"Your aunt is out of sorts because she's worried about her friend." Ross took up for her. "And she's a bit of a control freak."

The twins giggled as she shot him a glare and hurried out the door.

Once in the truck, silence echoed.

Ross backed out of the drive. "Which hospital?"

"The one in Boerne. It's about forty-five minutes. I just put it in my phone GPS. She's finding us."

"That's toward Bandera, right?" He hesitated at the end of the driveway.

"Yes."

"Sorry about the control freak remark." He pulled onto the highway. "I was trying to lighten things up a bit."

More silence.

Was she that mad at him? Or was it more than that? Her friend was about to have a baby. Something Stacia would never do if she followed her doctor's advice.

"This must be hard on you."

"I'm just nervous. Larae was in a lot of pain."

"I mean the whole baby thing."

"I'm very happy for Larae and Rance."

"But I imagine it's still hard."

"They had a rocky beginning and their daughter, Jayda, is eight now. But they fought their way to happily-ever-after and the new baby puts a much deserved exclamation point on their bliss." She let out a sigh. "But to be honest, her pregnancy has been a constant reminder that I'll never have that joy."

"Does she know?"

Stacia shook her head. "No one knows except Daddy. And you."

"And only because I badgered it out of you." He winced. "Sorry about that. But you should tell your friends. Isn't that what friends are for? To share your ups and downs."

"At first, it was too painful. I couldn't talk about it. It's still hard. But about the time I was ready to tell them, Larae broke the news about the baby. I didn't want to discourage her excitement or have her tiptoe around me." Her voice caught. "I just couldn't let her know that every bout of morning sickness, every craving, every kick makes me ecstatic for her. But at the same time, it hurts my soul." Guilt tinged her tone.

"You shouldn't beat yourself up for how you feel." He reached over, found her hand on the console, and squeezed it. "And you shouldn't suffer alone."

She stiffened, then relaxed for a few seconds before pulling her hand away.

Back to silence.

"You really should talk to someone."

"So now you think I need a shrink?"

"That's not what I meant." He gripped the steering wheel tight. Why did she take everything he said the wrong way? "Family, a friend, or your preacher. Anyone, just so it doesn't eat at you."

"I'm done talking about this with you."

"I only want to help you."

The silence turned deafening. The only interruption for the remainder of the drive was the monotone voice on her GPS giving directions.

By the time they pulled into the hospital lot, he was eager for escape. "I'll drop you at the door and find a parking spot."

"You can go on home. Lexie will probably be here. I can catch a ride with her or somebody else later."

"I'm not leaving until I know you have a ride."

"Fine."

As soon as he stopped the truck, she bailed out. Without so much as a thank-you. He was tempted to leave her to it. But as he watched her disappear through the door, with a pile of hurt and a heap of responsibility on her slight shoulders, he couldn't do it.

Instead, he pulled into the parking garage and drove the aisles until he found an open spot. He drew in a steadying breath and got out of the truck. Ready to be there if she needed a ride home.

Why did he care if she held everything inside until she blew or fell apart? The only things he knew for certain—she didn't trust him and he couldn't afford to care about her.

Stacia stepped in the waiting room to find Lexie in a chair with Jayda in her lap looking at something on her phone. Lexie's fiancé, Clint, sat beside her along with Lexie's parents, Stella and Denny. Her vision blurred and she blinked several times to keep the moisture at bay.

After Larae's mom died and then Stacia's, Stella had become like a second mom to both of them. The need to share her burden balled up in her chest.

"Any news?"

All eyes met hers.

"Everything's progressing just fine." Stella patted the empty seat beside her. "Did you drive here alone? We should have swung by to get you."

"I had to get the twins settled and Daddy thought I was too nervous to drive, so Ross brought me."

Lexie's eyebrows went up. "Where is he?"

"Parking the car. Can I catch a ride home with someone, so he can leave? He really needs to be manning the workshop, so Daddy can focus on the twins."

"Sure." Lexie squelched a yawn. "Clint and I will have to go home at a decent hour since I have to work tomorrow."

"But I don't want to leave." Jayda groaned. "Daddy said I could stay until my baby brother is born."

"Then you certainly will." Stella clapped her hands. "Denny and I are here for the long run."

"That is if you think your folks will let us shirk our ranch duties tomorrow." Denny winked at the little girl.

"He's here." Rance stepped into the doorway, grinning from ear to ear.

"Already?" Lexie jumped up as Jayda scampered off her lap and ran to her father.

Rance knelt to scoop her up. "Raymond Laurance Shepherd made his appearance at 5:15. Mommy and baby are both fine. He's twenty-two inches long and eight pounds, fourteen ounces. We're gonna call him Rand."

"Is Mommy okay?"

"Maybe a little tired, but other than that, she's just fine as fine can be. Wanna see your baby brother and then Mommy?"

Jayda clung to him. "Can we?"

"This way, everybody."

"We can all go?" Denny picked his cowboy hat up from the end table.

"For a few minutes."

"That was so fast." Lexie checked her watch. "I figured it would be hours."

"Second babies often come in a hurry." Stella stood. "Let's go see the little darlin'."

Stacia hung back, not trusting her emotions.

But Stella waved her on. The small crowd followed Rance with Stacia making up the tail.

A very tired Larae sat propped up in the bed holding a

newborn. A thatch of dark hair, a tiny red face, screaming his lungs out.

"Why's he crying, Daddy? Is he okay?" Jayda asked.

"He's just mad cause Mommy's tummy was warm and dark and cozy and he's not sure he's ready to be out here in the big, bright world." Rance scooped the baby up as Larae motioned their daughter over. Jayda carefully snuggled into the bed with her mom.

A hand landed on Stacia's shoulder. "You okay?" Stella's kind chocolate eyes inspected her.

Only then did she realize she was crying. She swiped at her cheeks. "Just happy for them."

"Me too." Stella hugged her.

"He's beautiful." Stacia kissed her friend's cheek, then stepped back so others could give their congrats. With no one paying attention, she eased out of the room. Needing air and time to compose herself, she made her way back to the waiting room.

Ross was there, flipping through a glossy magazine.

"You're still here."

He set the periodical aside. "I told you I wouldn't leave until I knew you had a ride. Everybody okay?"

"They're great. She had a boy, Raymond Laurance Shepherd. Rand for short, after Larae's dad, and Rance. And Laurance after Larae's mom, Laura, and Rance since his name is really Terrance." She was rambling. "Can we get out of here?"

"Sure."

He stood, followed her to the elevator. Three hospital staff members got on with them. As the doors slid closed, she texted Lexie that she'd forgotten to tell Ross he could go, so he was taking her home.

Once on the main floor, they made their way outside. "You could wait here while I get the truck."

"I'm fine."

"We're in the parking garage over there." He pointed and they headed in that direction.

She should thank him for waiting. But at the moment, if she said anything, she'd start blubbering. Instead they trudged to the cement structure and entered.

Seemingly miles later, she spotted his truck. It beeped when he clicked the fob.

Once inside, she buckled her seatbelt, leaned her head back, closed her eyes, and took deep breaths.

His hand covered hers.

But this time, she didn't pull away. "I was standing in Larae's room bawling my eyes out. How can I be so happy for my friend and so sad at the same time? I'm a horrible person."

"You're not. You're a person who's unable to have something you badly want."

"I don't know if I can do this. How can I hold her baby and act like I'm okay?"

"You have to tell her."

"But I don't want to put a damper on her happiness."

"If you don't tell her, she'll wonder why you cry every time you see her."

"I've held it together so far."

"But you can't keep bottling your feelings up."

"I don't. I pray about them."

"And that's great. But you're not being honest with your friends. And from what I've seen y'all are really close. How do you think they'd feel if they knew you were keeping this from them?"

"But I can't talk about it without crying." She clasped her hand to her mouth, but a little moan slipped out as tears coursed down her cheeks.

"I think they can handle it. And so can I." Ross leaned

toward her, and strong arms came around her. "Stupid console."

But she was glad it was there. He was way too close as it was as she soaked his shoulder and he awkwardly patted her hair.

How could Stacia act like nothing happened last night, while all Ross wanted to do was touch her hair again? It had been just as silky as he'd imagined and he'd had to force himself not to run his fingers through it all day.

She finished painting the coffee bar, pulled her mask down to under her chin and caught him staring. "What?"

"Um. I was, um, just thinking." He pulled his mask down as well, trying desperately to come up with something other than the truth. "Wondering if you're still sore."

"A little." She stretched her back. "But much better than it was."

Stop staring. "Isn't it about time for the twins to come home?" He checked his watch.

"It is. Mind if I open the doors, to help with the fumes?"

"Not at all."

"At least it's a little windy today. I'll be glad when October comes. But then this is Texas, it may not really cool off during the day until November. Or January." She opened the double doors and the breeze played with her hair.

"I wish—"

"What do you wish?"

That they could explore whatever made the air crackle between them. Was it them? Or just him? Think fast. Something to cover.

"That we all lived closer. It's all so complicated. My parents aren't the type to be long-distance grands. Especially since they've already missed five years of Mason and Madison's lives."

Something in her eyes softened. "You really don't want to hurt anyone involved, do you?"

"Nope. Especially not the kids."

"And you weren't trying to manipulate me with the whole Adrian happily-ever-after offer, were you?"

"Nope." In fact, he was pretty pumped that she didn't love Adrian. Even if he couldn't allow himself to fall for her. And she was making it tougher by going all soft, like she might could trust him.

"I'm sorry I'm so gun-shy. After my mom died, her sister came to stay with us and help Daddy. But it turned out, she wasn't anything like Mom. Aunt Eleanor was very manipulative and my experience with her makes it hard for me to trust people. But I'm trying."

Her phone made a sound and she checked it. "Looks like your background check came back clean."

"Just like I said it would." Could she find it in her heart to trust him now?

A knock sounded at the door from the store.

"That'll be the twins. Do you think it's okay for them to come in? I get so used to paint fumes, I can't tell."

How would he know? She made it hard for him to breathe.

He forced his focus from her and inhaled. "I think it's okay."

"Come in."

Mason burst through. "Look at the picture I drew. My teacher gave me a gold star."

They both met the boy as Madison followed him inside.

"That's Uncle Ross and that's you, Aunt Stacia, with me and Madison in the middle."

"This is really good." Ross inspected the drawing, typical stick figures in crayon. But the figures were all holding hands looking like a happy family. Just like he was beginning to wish they could be.

"Grandpa said Bluebell had her calf. Can we go see it now?" Madison asked.

"Let's go." Stacia took off her smock.

"Yay." Mason scurried for the open door.

Stacia followed with Madison, then stopped and turned back. "Want to join us?"

"More than anything. But what about the workshop?"

"It won't take long and we both could use a break."

"Come on, Uncle Ross," Madison called over her shoulder.

He followed the threesome, who'd become so important to him in such a short time. All three of them. But what could he do about that? He'd figure something out for him and his folks to be family with the twins. Stacia was a different subject. Could she ever trust him enough to explore a relationship with him? Or if he gave in to his developing feelings for her, would his heart get broken?

No. No. No. He'd been through this with Nora. Constantly trying to prove himself. Constantly trying to gain her trust. Constantly realizing he hadn't when she did a one-eighty on him. He couldn't go through that again. And besides that, he had to go back to Houston and help his folks with the store.

The part of the day when he was in the workshop with Maverick was beginning to be his favorite. They'd developed an easy rapport. So much easier than the constant tension between him and Stacia as he tried his best to guard his heart.

They stopped at the rail fence, where the cow grazed in the pasture with the calf close by.

"Can't we see him up close? Pleeeease," Mason begged.

"I don't know." Ross put plenty of caution in his tone. "Some mama cows are pretty protective. She might not like us getting any closer than this."

"Uncle Ross has a point." Stacia shrugged. "But I bottle-fed Bluebell after her mama died. This is her third calf and she hasn't minded us getting close so far."

"Just in case she has a change of heart, let me go first." Ross held his hands up, motioning for the twins to stay put. "I'll make sure it's safe." He climbed the fence, jumped down on the pasture side and slowly approached the cow. "Easy girl, we just want to see that fine baby you've got there."

"Uncle Ross loves us, doesn't he?" Madison said.

"He does." Stacia's agreement warmed his heart. "What makes you say that?"

"Because he wants to keep us safe, just like you do."

"You're very astute."

"What does that mean?" Mason asked.

Ross inwardly chuckled, then continued sweet-talking the cow. No show of aggression and he was almost on them.

"You should be able to pet her," Stacia coached from the sidelines.

"Hey pretty mama." Ross set his hand on the cow's back. She didn't stiffen or twitch. "You're just a big softy, huh?" He motioned for the twins. "She's calm, cool and collected."

The twins climbed over the fence and scampered toward him.

"Wc got a couple more coming to see your handsome fella."

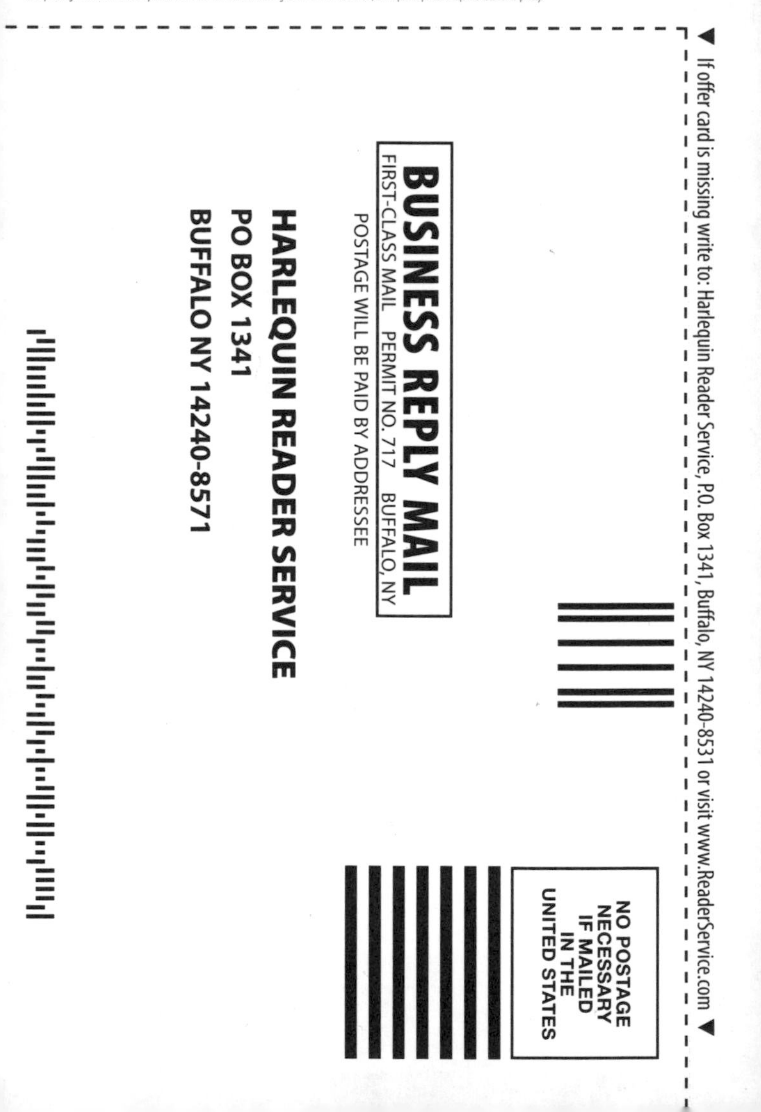
If offer card is missing write to: Harlequin Reader Service, P.O. Box 1341, Buffalo, NY 14240-8531 or visit www.ReaderService.com
BUSINESS REPLY MAIL
FIRST-CLASS MAIL PERMIT NO. 717 BUFFALO, NY
POSTAGE WILL BE PAID BY ADDRESSEE
HARLEQUIN READER SERVICE
PO BOX 1341
BUFFALO NY 14240-8571
NO POSTAGE NECESSARY IF MAILED IN THE UNITED STATES

Stacia stayed put. The farthest she'd been from him when he was with the twins.

Were they finally getting somewhere? But he couldn't let it go to his head. Or his heart.

Chapter Seven

It had been hard for Stacia watching from a distance as Ross and the twins interacted with the calf yesterday. But he was their uncle, and she needed to work at giving him free access to the twins, even if it killed her.

With the coffee bar she'd stayed to finish freshly painted, Ross still at the workshop and Daddy on twin duty, Stacia drove to Larae's.

Since her friend had been home from the hospital for a day, Stacia really should stop in and see the new baby. She wanted to. Just didn't trust her emotions, as she turned down the long drive. Hopefully, she'd cried all her tears out the night of little Rand's birth.

Stella's and Lexie's cars were parked by the house. Gripping the steering wheel, she drew in a deep breath and killed the engine.

Rance met her at the door, wearing an apron. "Hey Stacia. Come on in."

"I'm cooking supper with Daddy." Wearing a matching apron, Jayda squeezed around him.

"I see that."

"They're in the bedroom." Rance ushered her in. "You can go on up."

"And stay for supper." Jayda wiped her hands on her apron.

"I don't think so. We're going to Bible study and I promised the twins we'd eat at Dairy Queen in Bandera afterward. Maybe you could go with us."

The longing was there in Jayda's pale blue eyes. "No, I have to help Daddy with supper and Mama with the baby."

"If you're sure you don't mind, Stacia, we're good here. Jayda loves her Wednesday night class and there's no need for her to miss church. Or anything else."

"Mason and Madison would love for her to join us." As much as Larae had helped out with the twins, it felt good to return the favor.

"Good idea." Rance squeezed Jayda's shoulder. "Your mama and Rand will be here when you get back."

"Yes please." Jayda smiled.

"It's settled then." Rance ushered Jayda toward the kitchen.

"I'll come get you before I leave."

Stacia closed her eyes, drew in a calming breath and headed up the stairs. By the time she approached the open door of the master bedroom, she was all smiles.

"Hey everybody."

Larae reclined in the bed, propped on pillows, with Lexie holding little Rand and Stella sitting on a loveseat nearby.

"Hey." Larae reached for her hand.

"You doing okay?" She clasped her friend's fingers.

"Just sore and tired. But good. Really happy."

"I told her we don't care if she sleeps, since we didn't come to see her." Stella chuckled.

"Want to hold him?" Lexie asked.

"That's what I came for." She took the warm bundle from her friend, wrapped in blue with a little face peeking out. His eyes, framed by inky hair, matched his blanket. Would little Rand keep Larae's eyes or would they change to green like his dad's? Baby shampoo and sweetness wrapped up in tiny innocence.

She'd never have this. Never have a child to wonder if he or she would look like her or her husband. Since most men probably wanted kids eventually, she'd likely never have a husband, even if she eventually found a man she could trust.

"Are you okay, darlin'?" Stella handed her a tissue.

Oh dear. She dabbed her eyes. "I need to tell y'all something."

"What is it?" Stella patted the loveseat beside her. Always on alert at mothering all three of them, even though Lexie was her only child.

"I have the same heart defect that my mom and my sister had. My doctor recommended that I don't have children."

"Oh hon." Stella put an arm around her.

Stacia leaned on her stand-in mom's shoulder and let the tears come as Lexie swooped in to reclaim Rand.

"We suspected," Larae said.

"You did?" Her voice came out wobbly.

"Well with what happened to your mom and Callista. Childbirth was the common denominator."

"But we thought maybe we were wrong." Lexie shrugged. "You've always talked about getting married and having kids. Even since you've had the twins, you've mentioned having cousin siblings for them."

"Wishful thinking." Stacia pulled away from Stella and mopped her face with the tissue. "Doctors caught the defect when my mom died, and found mine and Calli's. But Daddy didn't tell us until we were a little older. I didn't want y'all to feel sorry for me. Or weird around me if one of you ever had a baby. Like you do now."

"We don't feel weird." Lexie perched on the loveseat arm next to her. "We love you."

"I'm really happy for you, Larae. I am."

"I know."

"Besides, I've got the twins. And if you two keep having babies, I'll have them to love and help mother the way Stella has mothered all of us."

"Whoa, I'm not even married yet." Lexie settled Rand into her shoulder.

"Can I hold him again?"

"Sure." Lexie handed him over. "And you can still get married someday, maybe adopt."

"In the meantime, whenever you need some sweet baby love, you know where to come." Larae shot her a wink. "But this was a lot easier when I was eighteen. So don't expect me to be a baby factory."

Stacia chuckled and kissed little Rand on the forehead, seeing him as the blessing he was.

The sound of Stacia's sander reached Ross before he ever stepped through the open back door of the workshop the next morning.

"The pregnant jersey didn't come to feed this morning, so I'm off to go hunt her up," he hollered.

"I hope she's okay." Stacia didn't turn off her tool or look up from her claw-foot tub project.

"Is this her first calf?"

"Yes. She might be protective. Take some range cubes to distract her with and call if you need help."

"I've got this. But thanks." No way would he let her think he couldn't handle a cow. Not with her just beginning to count on him. He hurried toward the barn.

He grabbed a blanket and tack from a stall, and tucked two handfuls of cubes in his pocket.

With a rope on his arm and the saddle against his hip, he opened the gate and clicked his tongue as he approached the buckskin filly assigned to him. She followed him out of the barnyard and stood still, flicking her black tail, as he fastened the gate, then approached her.

"Hey girl." He ran his hand down her golden face. "You're ready for another ride, aren't you?" He set the blanket and saddle on her back, tightened it in place and slipped the bridle over her head. The horse had trusted him like this the very first time he'd ridden her.

Unlike Stacia. But over the last several days, they'd jumped a few hurdles.

He slid his foot into the stirrup and the horse stood stock still as he mounted.

"Yah." He urged her into a canter, searching the edge of the woods as he rode. The jersey cow would blend in with the yellowed grass. Hard to find. He hoped if she'd had the calf or was in the process, coyotes hadn't found her.

Nothing. He followed the trail into the woods, crossed the river at a shallow point and searched the next field. Over by a cluster of large, round hay bales, he saw something move. Small. Either the calf or a coyote. He squeezed his heels into the buckskin's sides urging her into a full gallop.

As he neared, he was able to make out the calf with its mother close by, totally blending in with the bales. Still. Wary. He might have to call Maverick to distract her, so he could get to the calf. But no way would he call Stacia. He couldn't take the chance of shaking her burgeoning faith in him.

He led the horse to the farthest hay bale, dismounted

and made his way around the maze of bales to the cow's other side, then gingerly headed in her direction.

She made a gruff, growling sound—universally known to ranchers as mad mama moo. Oh boy. "Come on, little mama. I'm just trying to help. If y'all stay out here tonight, the coyotes will come and neither of us want that."

She took a few trotting steps toward him and he ducked behind a bale. The calf was no help; it stayed right under her.

"Just let me take your little darling back to the barn, so you'll both be safe. You can come too." He threw a cube toward her and she stooped to eat it. Then threw another, a little farther away. But the cow didn't fall for it. She did her mad mama moo again.

"Need some help?" Stacia called.

He looked up to see her astride her bay, one hand blocking the sun from her eyes.

"I've got this."

"I can tell, with you cowering behind a hay bale and all." Her mouth twitched.

She better not laugh. He might just have to—kiss her. Now, where did that come from? "I don't see you dismounting."

"I can't rope her if I dismount, now can I?"

"*You* can rope?"

"I suggest you get back on your horse and watch." She took her rope off her saddle horn.

"You're on." He rounded the bales and mounted the buckskin, then steered her to head off the cow.

Stacia rode her horse in closer until the cow trotted away, then swung the lasso in a circle above her head and released, capturing the cow's back hoof. She struggled, did her mad mama moo and the calf stayed under her as Stacia took up the slack in the rope.

With the cow distracted by tugging at the lasso, Ross dismounted, managed to fish the calf out from its mother's shelter, pick him up and haul him up onto the horse. As he settled in the saddle, thankfully, the calf didn't fight him.

The calf bawled and the mama did too as Stacia jumped down from her horse and ran to loosen the loop on the cow's heel.

"Careful there."

"She's not mad at me. You're the one who took her calf." She slapped the mad mama on the rump and the cow bolted away from her. Once she was back on her horse, he rode over beside her.

"Where'd you learn to do that?"

"I've helped Daddy with the ranch since I can remember. Calli never wanted anything to do with the cattle, but I tried to be Daddy's boy since he didn't have one."

"I'm impressed." But there was nothing boyish about her.

"I'm impressed you got the calf, with my help." She didn't quite manage to suppress a grin.

"I had it handled."

"Uh-huh, half a day later, maybe."

The cow's mournful bawl pierced the air.

"I know. But we're trying to help you," Stacia soothed.

They fell into a trot side by side back toward the barn with the cow following close behind. This was the most relaxed, easiest to be with Stacia he'd encountered since knowing her.

"I appreciate you getting the calf." Her gaze never strayed from the path ahead, though her horse knew the way. "I couldn't have done it on my own and I don't think Daddy, with his bad knee, could have lifted him onto his horse."

"Not a problem." He hadn't let her down after all. "Let's settle the calf and get back to work then."

Just because she halfway trusted him with the twins and a newborn calf, didn't mean she was ready to hand over her heart. He needed to treat her like the twins' aunt and nothing more. Or he could end up in a heap of hurt.

Another Saturday, with the kids out of school for the weekend, but she was stuck working. With Ross.

The door from the workshop opened and Daddy stepped through. "Good news. My salvage guys got a bid for tearing down two old hotels in Austin." He showed her a picture on his tablet with corbels galore all along the porch. "There are more than enough claw-foot tubs and old doors to complete the B and B order, so you and Ross won't have to make another scavenging run."

"That's wonderful. But kind of sad about the hotel." Such architectural detail deserved to be preserved.

"I agree. But we're making sure some of the pieces live on at least. Ms. Heathcott will love the history."

"When will they be here?"

"They're starting the job Monday. Should be done by Wednesday or Thursday."

"Perfect."

"Carry on." Daddy went back into the store.

"That's a really nice piece." Ross eyed the coffee bar she'd just painted, with Queen Anne legs and detail. "It might be my favorite. Except for the girly colors."

"It might be mine too. My mom loved Queen Anne and lavender. She'd love this."

"You haven't talked about her much."

"She was a great mom. I miss her." She pulled her goggles up on top of her head, tried to keep the quiver out of her voice. "The teen years are hard enough without losing your mom. Larae's mom died a little before mine did, so Stella became like a mother to the three of us. She tried with Calli, but she was just so angry after mom's death."

"And then you lost her in your twenties. You've had your share of grief. But instead of crumbling, I think it made you stronger."

"I had to be strong. For Mason and Madison." She caught his gaze, held it, then eyed the claw-foot tub she should be sanding instead of chitchatting with him. But this was more than idle prattle. Maybe if she gave him insight into her world, he'd see how important the twins were to her. "They've become my world. Especially since I can't have kids."

"I can see that."

"I do have some respect for your brother's generosity." She never asked for a dime, but the checks just started coming. "Even though his financial responsibility ended when he signed custody over to Calli." She glanced his way for half a second. "The checks still come and I can assure you that every penny is spent on Mason and Madison or deposited into their trust fund accounts I set up. I can show you the bank statements."

"No need. I can tell you're not living the lavish lifestyle. And I trust you."

He trusted her? The feeling definitely wasn't mutual. Not completely anyway.

"I'd say it's hush money, except that scandal feeds Ron's career. So maybe for once in his life, he's taken responsibility." Sadness coated Ross's tone.

It was obvious that his brother's actions had hurt him too. "I've always been terrified he'd change his mind someday and come to claim them."

"That's one worry you can put to rest."

"I always wondered if he was telling the truth about

not having any family. I mean, everybody has parents. I thought a lot about them over the years—if they knew about the twins, if they cared."

"I can see how imagining Ronny Outrageous with stable, Christian parents is difficult." He paused in his work, dropped his gaze to the dusty concrete floor. "But I can assure you if they'd known, they'd have been a part of Mason's and Madison's lives from the beginning."

He didn't even try to stand up for his brother, plead his case. But Ron was Ron. And apparently Ross had come to terms with it.

"I thought about trying to find out, but I was terrified of losing the twins."

"You're doing a great job with them. My parents will want to be grandparents. But I'm pretty sure that's all. Callista left them with you."

Raised in church, with both parents. The way Ron had turned out didn't make any sense. Yes, Calli had gone through a wild stage, but she was reeling from their mom dying. Maybe someday, Ron would return to his raising, the way Calli had in her last few years. But if Ron accepted Jesus, would he want the twins?

"I'll do anything to keep Mason and Madison." Her voice cracked. "Your parents can visit as often as they want."

"It'll all work out. As long as we're all willing to compromise."

"When do you plan to tell them?"

"I figure it needs to be done in person. But I feel obligated to stay here until the B and B order is complete. After that, I'll go home and break the news."

"I need some air." She jerked the goggles over the back of her head, but the strap snarled in her hair at the base of her neck. "Ouch."

"Here, let me." His hand grazed hers as he gently took the goggles from her, easing the weight on her hair. His knuckle skimmed her shoulder.

Too close. "Just cut it."

"I've almost got it. Just be still." His breath fanned her neck as his fingers brushed against sensitive skin.

She gasped as his proximity sent a shudder through her. No. No. No. Yes, he was ridiculously handsome. No, she couldn't trust him. Even though she was starting to want to. But she *could not* be attracted to him.

"There. Got it." He pulled the goggles away, let her hair fall.

"Thanks." She turned just enough to take the safety glasses from him. Too far.

His green gaze locked on hers, then dropped to her lips.

She bolted, slammed the door behind her, dragging in big gulps of air. No. No. No. She could not fall for Ross Lyles.

What if he was pulling an Aunt Eleanor on her? Resorting to romance to finagle the twins away from her? She couldn't fall for his ploy.

Chapter Eight

Sunday never lasted long enough. And Monday always followed. If only Daddy could paint, Stacia could be in the park with the twins instead of stuck in the workshop with Ross. But Daddy had never learned how to operate the sprayer without causing drips on whatever he painted.

Tension dripped between them after yesterday's too-close encounter. How could one day in the workshop feel like an entire week? An entire week of silence. She couldn't take it any longer.

Her phone rang, rescuing her from the deafening hush. Daddy.

"Hello?"

"Now don't freak out."

Her heart went into orbit. "I already am when you start a phone call like that."

"The kids are fine. But I tried to push them on the merry-go-round and I've twisted my knee. I'm not sure I can drive home."

"I'm on my way." She ended the call and slid her phone back in her pocket.

"What's wrong?"

The first conversation Ross had instigated all day. She filled him in.

"I'll go with you."

"There's no need." She didn't want to be stuck in her SUV with him.

"Somebody needs to drive Maverick's truck home."

Made sense. She held in a sigh, grabbed her purse. "Okay."

Ross matched her stride as she hurried to her vehicle. She started the engine as he crawled in the passenger side. His cologne filled her space. Spicy and manly.

"I have to admit, my hat's off to you and Maverick." Ross fastened his seatbelt as she pulled out of the drive.

"For?"

"For handling the twins, just the two of you up until now."

"There's only two of them and there's two of us." What was he getting at? That they needed him and his family to help? "We manage fine."

"I know. I see that. But before I came, what would you have done today?"

"I'd either have taken one of our employees, or locked Daddy's truck up and left it until Larae or somebody could go with me to get it." Lexie, Clint, Rance. Anybody other than Ross. Why hadn't she insisted on him staying at the workshop?

"I hope you'll come to realize that my folks can be a help to you, just like I can. What if you and Maverick got sick at the same time?"

"We hardly ever get sick. And Larae and Lexie have been able to help since they moved back to Medina."

"And before then?"

"We managed." *We don't need any help.*

"You don't always have to do everything on your own,

Stacia. Especially not with me here. And even more so, once my folks know about the twins."

Maybe she liked doing things on her own. Not depending on anyone else. That way, she didn't get disappointed. Or hurt.

Conversation died and uncomfortable silence took over for the rest of the fifteen-minute drive.

When she turned into the park, she saw Daddy sitting on a bench with the kids playing nearby. Daddy was only sixty. But years of hauling furniture and salvaging buildings had taken a toll on him. He was slowing down. Eventually, he'd need knee replacement surgery.

She parked, got out of the car and ran over to Daddy. "Can you walk?"

"With some help. I'm glad you brought Ross. I'll need both of you to keep the weight off my knee."

"Here, let me help you up." Ross sat down by Daddy on his right, his bad knee side. "Let's take it slow, lean on me."

Daddy put his arm around Ross's shoulder and stood with a slight moan. With his weight supported mostly by Ross, Stacia took his good knee side. With his other arm around her shoulder, they hobbled toward the SUV.

Okay, so it would be easier with Ross to get Daddy home. And it was hard taking care of the twins. Even with both of them healthy. But they'd managed. She didn't need someone else swooping in and trying to take over. Or even worse, taking them away.

And now that there was a timeline on when his parents would learn the truth, her fears multiplied.

Giggling caught Ross's attention and he looked up from the coffee bar. Madison zipped past the open workshop doors with Mason close behind.

"Is this what they did over the summer?" He'd much rather be playing with the twins than working with the aunt he couldn't let himself fall for.

"Occasionally. But most days, if we were fully staffed, Daddy and I took turns corralling them."

At least they were easily entertained and there hadn't been much arguing.

With Maverick laid up from his knee injury yesterday, the kids had to stick around the workshop after school. With the double doors on the back of the shop open, the twins could scurry about just outside and avoid the paint fumes. While Ross assembled coffee bars and sanded claw-foot tubs, Stacia was on paint duty for both.

"Madison, watch out!" Mason shouted.

A heart-splitting scream echoed through the air.

Ross ran toward the sound, but somehow Stacia beat him to the little girl sprawled on the ground, cradling her left arm.

"What hurts?" Stacia knelt over her.

"She fell, but her arm landed on that prickly pear cactus." Mason pointed at the paddle-shaped plant covered in needles.

Stacia closed her eyes. "Let me see."

Ross knelt on Madison's other side. Big tears rolled down her sweet little cheeks. He smoothed her hair away from her face as she showed them her arm. Multiple spines dotted the tiny wrist.

"We'll have to go to the doctor, Mad. He'll get them out and everything will be just fine."

Whimpering softly, Madison nodded.

"Keep your wrist from touching anything, so they won't get mashed in deeper, and I'll carry you." Ross scooped the child up into his arms, then caught Stacia's gaze. "Just get Mason into my truck."

As Madison curled into his chest, amazingly, Stacia didn't argue. She climbed in the back between the two car seats, then helped Mason buckle his as Ross gently sat Madison in hers. Except he didn't know where her doctor's office was. "Where am I going?"

"Bandera."

The longest fifteen-minute drive of his life, with constant moans and whimpers coming from the back seat. Mason was the quietest Ross had ever seen him.

Ross caught his eye in the rearview mirror. "She'll be okay, bud. I stepped on a prickly pear when I was a kid. It hurt like crazy, but the doctor got them all out, and I was good as new." He spared the digging around with tweezers one at a time process Madison would have to endure.

Finally, he followed Stacia's directions and pulled into the lot of the Bandera Medical Clinic and parked, then flung his door open. By the time he opened Madison's door, Stacia had her unbuckled. He picked Madison up and she wrapped her good arm around his neck.

"It's okay, sweet pea. You'll feel better soon."

Stacia scurried ahead, opened the door for him, then signed Madison in while he settled in a chair. The child clung to him with her good arm as her tears dripped onto his neck. If the doctor didn't get them in soon, he'd be crying too.

Only a few other patients dotted the room. Maybe it wouldn't be long. Stacia sat down beside him and Mason clambered into her lap. She leaned her head against Madison's with her shoulder against his and murmured comforting words.

The door to the exam rooms opened and a nurse scanned the waiting room. "Madison Keyes."

Keyes. Her name should be Lyles. He jumped to his feet and hurried toward the nurse.

"Room 2." She pointed the way.

"I don't want to go," Mason said.

Ross turned to check on Stacia. Both were still in the waiting room with Mason shaking his head.

"Maybe Dad can get her settled, then stay with the boy and Mom can go in with Madison." The nurse smiled.

"We're not married," his voice blended with Stacia's.

Great, now the nurse thought they were shacked up, having kids together.

"We share a niece and nephew." He turned to Stacia. "Mason, just come back with us long enough to get Madison settled, then I'll bring you back to the waiting room and stay with you."

Mason's chin trembled, but he complied.

"You can set Miss Madison on the exam table." The nurse gestured to the room. "And we'll take real good care of her. Let me see that arm, Madison."

The little girl bravely stuck her wrist out.

"I had a fight with a prickly pear when I was about your age," the nurse said. "It's like a rite of passage for Texans."

"What's a rite of passage?" Madison asked.

At least the nurse had her mind off her pain.

A small hand wiggled into his, gave a slight tug. He didn't want to leave, but Mason was obviously holding him to his word.

"We'll be right outside. Text me. Keep me posted."

"I will." Stacia nodded as the nurse tried to explain rite of passage to a kindergartener. "Will you let Daddy know what's going on?"

"Sure." Holding Mason's hand, Ross trudged back to the waiting room. As soon as he sat down, Mason crawled into his lap and pressed his cheek into Ross's chest. And even deeper into his heart.

"Hey bud, it's okay. She's gonna be fine." He texted Maverick a quick message.

"I pushed her." Mason's voice was thick with unshed tears. "That's why she fell into the pricklers."

"Oh bud, you didn't mean to hurt her, did you?"

"No. But we'd seen the pricklers. I knew they were there."

"Why did you push her?"

"Because she's faster than me. And it makes me mad. But I didn't mean to hurt her."

"Of course you didn't. And Madison doesn't mean to be faster than you. It's just the way God made her." Ross stroked the child's hair stirring up the scent of shampoo, sweat and dirt—all boy. "But as you get older, you might get faster than her. My brother was faster than me when we were your age, but in high school, I got to where I could outrun him."

"You mean our dad?"

"The only brother I've got." He hadn't meant to go there. "Just remember this, the next time you get mad at Madison and you want to push her, she could get hurt and then you'd feel bad like you do now."

"Okay."

Maybe he'd managed to derail the conversation about Ron. If only Ron knew what he was missing.

"Wanna see the new game I put on my phone?" Ross pressed a kiss on top of Mason's head.

A message icon popped up at the top of the screen and he opened it.

They're out.

"See. Madison will be just fine now." He breathed a sigh of relief and opened the game.

* * *

Holding Madison's good hand, Stacia opened the door into the waiting room. Mason was sitting in Ross's lap, enthralled with something on his phone. Ross looked up and smiled at Madison.

"She was so brave."

"I'm sure she was." The lines across Ross's forehead faded away.

"Did they get 'em all out?" Mason clambered off his uncle's lap.

Ross stood and met them midway.

"We think so." Stacia headed for the exit. "But the doctor gave us a prescription for antibiotics and ointment just in case. That way if there are any left, they won't cause an infection. So we need to stop by the pharmacy on the way home." Her least favorite place in the world. Where some of her worst memories and nightmares had begun.

"How'd they get 'em?" Mason looked his sister's wrist over as they strolled toward the truck.

"They used a big sticky glove thingy. Just brushed it over my arm and the stickers stuck to it instead of in me."

"Cool." Mason climbed up into the truck.

"Remember not to get it against anything if you can help it." Stacia took her spot in the middle of the back seat.

"When I was a kid, they had to get them out one at a time with tweezers." Ross helped Mason into his car seat. "I'm glad they've made improvements in the process. Where's the pharmacy?"

"Just a little farther into town." Stacia buckled Madison in.

"I'm sorry I pushed you." Mason sniffled. "I didn't mean for you to fall into the pricklers."

"It's okay," Madison mumbled.

"Wait. You pushed Madison?" Stacia turned to her nephew.

"We already talked about it," Ross said from the front seat.

She looked up, caught his gaze in the rearview mirror.

"Mason knows now that if he pushes Madison or anybody else, they could get hurt. And he doesn't like feeling guilty, so he won't do it again. Right, bud?"

"Right."

"That's good." Stacia ruffled Mason's hair. "But I knew that prickly pear was there. I should have taken the time to dig it up."

"It's okay, Aunt Stacia. You've been busy." Madison inspected her reddened wrist. "I wonder why God made cactus?"

"Well they make pretty flowers. People in Mexico eat prickly pears and I think they have nutrients and vitamins that are good for you." Digging up the prickly pear would have taken two minutes, tops. She shouldn't have been too busy for that. "So if it gets really dry and everybody's garden dies, cactus can still live and we could eat them."

"And get pricklers in our bellies?" Mason grimaced.

"No silly." Stacia gently tapped his nose. "You have to peel the outer part off and just eat the fruit inside. But don't try it, they're hard to peel without getting stickers in your hands. The pharmacy is just ahead."

"I see it." Ross pulled into the lot, turned to face her. "I'll stay here with the kids."

Her nerve endings went taut. The exact scenario Aunt Eleanor had pulled. And as soon as Daddy stepped inside the pharmacy to pick up medicine for his bronchitis, Eleanor had sped away. With Stacia and Calli in the car.

"I'm not going anywhere." Ross's gaze locked on hers. "I promise. We'll be right here when you get back. I want

Madison to have her medicine and they both need all of their family members."

"Hurry, Aunt Stacia, I want to go home. My arm stings." Madison leaned her head back, closed her eyes.

"Okay, I'll be back in a jiff." Stacia patted Madison's good arm, then gingerly crawled around her car seat to get out.

Please don't let this be a mistake, Lord. Let them be here when I get back. She hurried across the parking lot, looking back several times. Each time, Ross and the twins were still there.

Inside, she prayed the entire time the pharmacist filled the prescriptions along with frequent checks at the window.

Ten minutes later, she stepped outside. The truck was still there. *Thank You, Lord.* When she opened the door, both twins were sleeping. Instead of taking the chance of disturbing them, she quietly shut the door and got in the front.

"Just call me the twin whisperer." Ross shot her a grin and started the engine.

"They've had a big day. Thanks for—" She didn't really know how to say it.

"Not kidnapping them?" He backed out, pulled onto the highway.

"That. And for carrying Madison and helping with Mason at the doctor's office."

"I love them too."

She believed him on that. It was both comforting and terrifying.

"It's no fun here without Madison." Mason stood just outside the open workshop doors, looking up at the sky, his shoulders slumped. "I'm *sooooo* bored."

Since Madison had stayed home from school, she was inside taking care of Maverick. It made Ross feel better to have them looking out for each other. But with school out now, Mason was at loose ends. At least the prickly pear was gone. Stacia had dug it up yesterday after they'd returned from the pharmacy.

"Maybe you'll learn to appreciate her." Stacia chuckled. "And it'll be church time before you know it."

"Do y'all have to work? Can't we do something fun until church? I heard Uncle Ross say y'all are ahead on the order."

"He's right. I did say that." Ross looked up from the coffee bar he was constructing. "What do you say I take Mason somewhere? That way, you could catch up on painting. We can't complete the order until everything's painted."

Indecision wrestled in her pale aqua eyes.

"Please Aunt Stacia. I'm *sooooo* bored."

"Okay." She pinned Ross with an intensely fierce look. "Just tell me what you plan to do, where you're going and when you'll be back."

"What do you want to do, bud?" Ross waggled his eyebrows.

"Can you teach me to ride a bike?" Mason ducked his head. "I mean without the training wheels. All the boys in my class can do it."

Ross caught Stacia's gaze. Failure lurked there.

"I'm not sure if that's a good idea, bud. Your aunt Stacia or your grandpa might want to teach you that."

"It's okay." Her tone didn't sound convincing. "Daddy and I have taught Mason lots of things and witnessed most of his and Madison's firsts. I guess it's your turn."

Wow. She was really trying to share the twins. Impressive. Had he finally managed to gain her trust yesterday?

Don't count on it. No falling for Stacia. She was the twins' aunt and he was their uncle. That's all. He couldn't risk letting anything happen between them because deep down, she'd never fully trust anyone and his parents needed him in Houston.

"I tell you what, I'll work with Mason a bit and when I think he's ready, I'll give you a holler. Maverick too. That way we all can be a part of this guy's big day."

"That sounds wonderful." Something in her tone softened. As if he'd given her a rare gift.

"All right. Come on Mason. Let's get this party started." Ross shot her a wink and ushered the boy outside. "Where's your bike?"

"In the garage."

"Lead the way."

"You really think I can do this in one day?"

"I sure do. You're you and I'm me. We've got this."

"Did you teach my dad to ride a bike?"

Ross's heart sank. The one subject he didn't want to get into. "No. My dad did that. He taught us both."

"Is he still alive?" Mason peered up at him. "My other grandpa."

Okay, make that two subjects. It was past time for his parents to be in the know. "He sure is. Your grandma too."

"Where are they? How come they haven't visited us yet?"

"In another part of Texas. I haven't told them about you and Madison just yet."

"Why not? Don't they like kids?"

"They love kids, but your aunt Stacia and grandpa Maverick aren't used to y'all having any other family members. I guess I was just trying to give them time to get used to everything. We'll see them soon though."

Was Stacia on board with that? Yesterday, they'd seemed to jump another hurdle.

Mason darted around the side of the garage attached to the farmhouse and Ross followed. Through the side door, he found the boy astride a red bike dotted with checkerboard winners' flags.

"Hop off and I'll get those extra wheels off there."

"How will I ride without them?"

"I'll help you, don't worry."

Mason climbed off, then squatted beside Ross as he loosened the bolts and slipped the training wheels off.

"Okay, hop on." Ross held the bike steady.

The boy swallowed hard.

"I won't let you fall. I promise."

Mason grinned and climbed on. "I can't wait to tell my friends at school."

"Just pedal, like you normally would."

They wobbled out of the garage.

"I don't know, Uncle Ross. This is hard."

"You just need a little practice."

Heavy on the right side, steady for a second, then Mason's weight transferred to the left. Ross kept him stable, trotting behind. Back and forth, they went up and down the driveway—only stopping when store customers pulled in or left.

After at least a dozen tries, Ross felt Mason's weight balance and steady.

"I think you're ready."

"I do too."

"You felt that?"

"Mmm-hmm."

"Okay, let's stop right here at the end of the drive and I'll call your grandpa."

Mason stopped and put his right foot on the ground

as Ross dug his phone out and tapped his address book, then strolled over to the open doors of the workshop. Stacia glanced his way and he gave her a thumbs-up, just as Maverick answered.

"Hey, Maverick, can you and Madison watch out the window? Mason has something to show everyone."

"Sure."

The curtain moved aside in the family room. Madison waved at him and he could see Maverick sitting beside her as Stacia stepped around the side of the workshop so she could watch.

"Here we go, bud." Ross pocketed his phone and gripped the back of the bike with his heart in his throat. What if Mason fell or got hurt?

"I'm kind of nervous with everybody watching."

"You've got this. We both felt it. Just do it again."

"You won't let go if I can't?"

"I won't. But if you're doing it and I let go, don't freak out. Just keep riding. When you get to the end of the drive, you can either turn and come back or stop. You ready?"

"Yep." Mason took his foot off the ground, put it on the pedal.

"Here we go."

A little wobbling and then Mason found his balance. Ross let go, held his breath, as Mason kept going without him. All the way to the end of the driveway and then came to a flawless stop, then steadied himself with one foot on the ground.

"Yeehaw!" Ross shouted as his chest swelled.

"I did it!"

"You sure did!" Stacia hollered, clapping her hands.

Ross hadn't felt such euphoria since he'd learned to ride when he was a kid. He turned to Stacia, picked her up and swung her around. With her hands resting on his shoulders, she laughed. As he set her down, her hands slid to his wrists. Their gazes locked.

"Do you think I can come back by myself?" Mason asked.

"I think you can." Stacia backed away from him, peered down the driveway.

Mason turned the bike to face them and lifted his foot off the ground as Ross held his breath again. A bit of wobbling ensued, but Mason found his balance and pedaled toward them.

"Look at you go." Stacia let out a whoop. "All by yourself."

Mason's grin was as wide as his face. And it made Ross's heart dance. Or was it Stacia's nearness? For the first time, they were like two proud parents. A team. Or maybe more.

Chapter Nine

Their day in the workshop had been productive, especially since the salvage guys had delivered the promised load from the hotel early that morning. With plenty of materials, they focused on their work, no conversation. Even more tension vibrated between them since Ross had gotten all caught up in Mason's achievement yesterday and made the mistake of embracing Stacia.

His phone rang and Stacia turned her sander off.

He fished it out of his pocket and scanned the screen. "Hey Mom."

"Hey stranger. Have y'all been watching the news?"

"Uh no. Been too busy." Supposedly helping Papaw with the ranch in Hondo.

"There's a tropical storm brewing into a hurricane and if it holds its current pattern and intensity, it could hit Houston next week."

His heart took a dive. "I'll come home."

"No. We've got things covered here. Miss Cotton's grandson is taking a semester off, so he's helping out. We'll probably get evacuated and end up there with y'all in Hondo anyway."

Only he wasn't there. He really needed to go home. It was time to tell them. And he couldn't do it over the phone.

"Let me talk to Daddy." Mom's voice interrupted his thoughts.

"Uh, I, he's not with me at the moment." Maybe she wouldn't call Papaw now and find out Ross hadn't been there.

"I tried the house but didn't get an answer. Well, I better get back to packing stuff up. Watch the weather."

"I will. Keep me posted on y'alls plans."

"Bye sweetheart."

"Bye Mom." He ended the call, slid his cell back in his pocket, closed his eyes. He hated lying to her.

"Is something wrong?" Stacia peered up at him.

"Just a potential hurricane aimed at Houston."

"Oh dear. Will your parents be okay?"

"It may fizzle out. If not, they'll probably have to evacuate."

"I imagine this won't be the first time."

"No. In the thirteen years since their store opened, Ike and Harvey have pummeled them with major damage and flooding."

"Do you need to go home? I mean to help them out?"

All ready to be rid of him, was she? He would feel better if he could help his folks batten down the hatches and move the most unique, hardest to replace furnishings into the second level of the store. But he couldn't. Not until he finished the B and B order.

"If the storm continues according to projections, I might." It helped nothing for him to have feelings for Stacia. He had to tamp them down and focus. "I'll know sometime next week."

"Don't let us keep you."

"We may need to wrap the order up sooner, so we can

get it shipped sooner than planned. If a hurricane hits, we could be in store for hail, tornadoes or flooding in Medina."

"I'm not sure we can do that, unless we don't sleep. It'll be fine as long as we can get everything secured in the delivery truck. Just in case we get any damage to the workshop." She cocked her head to the side, looking way too cute for his comfort. "If you don't mind me asking, where do they think you are? I mean, I couldn't help overhearing. She obviously thought you were with someone she knows."

"At my grandparents' ranch. In Hondo."

"So all this time they thought you were with your grandparents?"

"I visit often to do appraisals for Nanny and help during harvest time." He shrugged. "So when I found out about the twins, I told my folks I needed to go help Papaw."

"Don't they talk to each other?"

"Not as much as they'd like. Papaw's busy with the harvest this time of year and Mom and Dad are busy with Christmas orders for the store."

A knock sounded at the door from the store.

Stacia checked her watch. "I know who that is. Come in."

"Uncle Ross." Mason blasted into the workshop. "All the boys think I'm so cool because my training wheels are gone."

"Awesome." Ross gave him a high five.

"Guess what happened at school today." Madison followed her brother.

"What?"

"The meanest boy in our class—"

"Put a tack on the teacher's chair," Mason finished.

"They still do that these days?" Ross frowned.

"In kindergarten?" Stacia shook her head. "Well, I hope he gets punished. That hurts."

"You've sat on a tack?" Madison winced.

"The meanest boy in school put it on my chair."

"Have you ever sat on a tack, Uncle Ross?" Mason asked.

"No." He gave them a sheepish grimace.

"You put tacks on people's chairs?" Mason grinned.

"Just once. It was a terrible idea. Not mine. I was actually dared to do it because I was a rule follower." By his brother, their father. "I got detention for it and that was the last rule I ever broke. After that it didn't matter how much the other kids teased me."

"Aunt Stacia's a rule follower too." Madison giggled.

"If you follow the rules, you avoid trouble." Ross winked. "Trust me."

"That sounds like very good advice." For once Stacia agreed with him. "No tacks on chairs. Do you hear me, Mason?"

"Yes ma'am." But the boy couldn't contain an eye roll.

"If anyone around here ever does that, it would mean no side-by-side. Right?"

"Right." Both twins agreed.

But they all knew Mason was the weak link.

"How was your wrist today?"

"Fine." Madison showed it to them. "It feels normal."

Thankfully, it seemed okay. No signs of irritation or redness.

The door from the store opened and Maverick strolled in. "Okay kiddos, we're off. Can you cover the store for me, Stace?"

"Of course. Where are y'all going?" Stacia asked, with a note of longing in her tone.

Longing to escape him? Or be with the twins? Maybe both.

"We're going to the dude ranch over in Bandera. The twins want to fit in some bowling or maybe putt-putt."

"I'm not sure your knee is up to that." Her longing echoed louder at the mention of putt-putt.

Maybe it wasn't him.

"Why don't you go with them and let Maverick stay here?" Ross suggested it for himself as much as her, eager to escape the tension in the workshop.

"You do love putt-putt." Madison grabbed Stacia's hand and tugged.

"But I need to work here since I have to leave early anyway for Lexie's rehearsal later tonight. And I won't be here most of the day tomorrow because of the wedding."

"I can sit down and sand. Tonight and tomorrow." Maverick took the sander from her. "You go. Have fun."

"Come on, Aunt Stacia." Mason grabbed her other hand. "I can't beat Grandpa, but I can beat you."

"We'll see about that," she challenged as she slipped her goggles and apron off, then pointed a finger at her dad. "Only sanding."

"Aye, aye Captain." Maverick saluted her.

"Are you going to the wedding tomorrow night, Uncle Ross?" Madison asked.

"As a matter of fact, Clint invited me when we were in class last Sunday."

"Good." Madison clapped her hands. "I want you to see my new dress."

"We need to get moving, Mad." Stacia grabbed her purse.

The twins scurried toward him. Ross's heart swelled as the warm little bodies took turns embracing him. So accepting of him in their lives. If only their aunt could be.

* * *

They'd managed to get ahead of schedule yesterday, allowing Stacia to concentrate on Lexie's wedding. All of the rehearsing last night along with months of planning for a ceremony that was over in ten minutes.

But the ceremony had been sweet and adorable, beginning with Clint's niece, Charlee, walking down the aisle, throwing rose petals. Right on cue, but all in one big clump and she was done. Though she kept digging in her basket for more until she'd made it to the front of the church. Her brother, Cooper, had raced down the aisle with a precarious hold on the satin pillow holding Lexie's ring.

But the ceremony and vows had gone off without a hitch. Of course, as she'd stood at the front of the church behind Larae, Ross was right in her line of vision. She'd pretty much missed the vows. Afterward, she'd stood in the receiving line as a wave of well-wishers consisting of church family, friends and townspeople she'd known her entire life kept flowing through.

A lengthy photography session later, she'd thrown birdseed at a blissful Lexie and Clint as they'd dashed to his truck to begin their life together.

She was so happy for her friend. But the day put a pang in her heart. She'd never be a bride or some guy's everything.

"You out of here?" Larae had her sleek figure back in two weeks' time of giving birth.

"I'm on a mission for punch before I dry up and blow away. See y'all later." She pressed a kiss on little Rand's cheek, then made her way to the fellowship hall.

With only the cleaning crew left, consisting of Lexie's family and church family, Stacia slipped off her nude heels, giving her aching feet a reprieve. The shoes were comfortable—for heels. They didn't pinch anywhere, but the balls of her feet were done.

The poppy-red chiffon fluttered around her knees as she walked. Lexie's favorite, but she'd worked hard to find a shade that didn't clash with Stacia's hair. It was trendy and fashionable, a testament to Lexie's excellent taste. She'd definitely wear the dress again.

"There you are," Ross said.

She stopped but her nylon clad feet didn't, careening her into a skid on the polished concrete floor. He jumped up from the table where he sat and grabbed her shoulders. Once she was steady, she stepped back. His hands fell to his sides.

"Nice dance move. Sorry. I didn't mean to startle you."

Her cheeks warmed. "Why are you still here?"

"Your dad and the twins rode with me. But Maverick's knee was hurting, though he'll never admit it, and the twins were restless. He took your SUV since it's easier for him to get in and out of it. So instead of leaving you my truck, I stayed to collect you."

"Collect me? Like a sack of grain?"

"Drive you home. You don't look anything like a sack of grain."

And her face grew hotter. "Well, I am tired and my feet are done, so I kind of feel like one and I'm ready to be collected."

"Punch?"

Her gaze locked on the clear plastic cup filled with frothy red liquid. "I'd kill for that."

"It's all yours." He held both hands up as if surrendering.

She gulped the liquid down, trying not to completely lose all her manners.

"Have you eaten anything today?"

"No and I'm famished, but we need to get back to the workshop. I'll grab a sandwich when we get home."

"Stella's heating up some meatballs. There's also Mexican pinwheels, some other little hoity-toity hors d'oeuvre thingy with green and white stuff on a cracker like women like and a fancy-schmancy little sandwich with no crust."

His descriptions dragged a smile to her mouth.

"More punch?"

"And water. I think I'm on my way to dehydration. But I can get it."

"Stay put. I'll get it."

"Here you go, love." Stella set a plate in front of her. The hors d'oeuvre with the green stuff turned out to be a toasted cracker with cream cheese and chives.

"Oh Stella, have I ever told you how much I love you?"

"You have, darling. But save some of that love for Ross. He's the one who made you a plate." Stella headed back to the kitchen. "Might ought to nab him before some other gal does."

It wouldn't do any good to protest. "Let me wolf this down and I'll help you clean."

"No need." Stella waved her off. "I've got plenty of help and Lexie said something about you having a huge B and B order. Eat and get out of here."

She forked a meatball and sank her teeth into it, closed her eyes. Possibly the best thing she'd ever eaten. Ross returned balancing two cups of punch and a bottled water.

"Here you go." He set the drinks in front of her, reclaimed his seat across from her.

"Thank you. I mean—really. I was about to die of thirst and hunger."

"Well now, we can't have that, can we? My niece and nephew love you to pieces, so we gotta keep you going for them. Eat up."

"Any news on the potential hurricane?"

"Still building."

"We're ahead of schedule. I figure we can finish the order by Wednesday and get everything loaded safely in the truck."

"I hope you're right. I can't wait to wrap this up."

Did he mean the order? Or being stuck with her? Probably both. Along with telling his parents the truth.

He stood. "I'm gonna help the ladies clean."

Once he got in the kitchen, a few protests echoed through the fellowship hall and then girlish giggles from women old enough to be his grandmother.

Was Ross a charming con artist? Or was he sincere? If he was for real, she was missing out on something great. But there was no way to tell, without possibly getting very hurt.

And no matter how great or real he might turn out to be, she still couldn't have kids. And she'd heard him tell Madison he wanted them someday. Her heart stuttered at the reminder.

After meeting their quota in the workshop on this very long Saturday, Ross had taken the twins for a ride on the side-by-side. Stacia's nerves had been on edge, but she'd prayed through it. They'd returned right on time for supper and she'd been so relieved, she'd invited him to share in their meal.

She stirred the spaghetti sauce and dabbed her forehead with the back of her hand. September had turned into October without much difference in temperatures. Still mid to high eighties.

It wasn't like he hadn't eaten with them before, but it was the first time she'd willingly done the inviting. She couldn't stop thinking about the wedding. With the twins out of the picture and away from work, they'd been more at ease with each other. Relaxed and friendly.

Almost flirty.

Her cheeks heated at the memory. Maybe she'd just been too hungry to keep her guard up but Ross seemed to be proving himself and putting her fears at ease. And she couldn't deny the awareness between them.

But it couldn't go anywhere. He was here only for the twins and he obviously loved kids. Even if he turned out to be trustworthy, she still couldn't have kids. Which meant they had no future. She had to keep reminding herself of that. Every time he looked her way.

Mason bolted into the kitchen. "Is it ready yet? I'm starving."

"Almost. Wash your hands, then go ahead and set the table."

He stretched over the sink and soaped his hands good, then grabbed the stool they kept in the pantry and climbed up to get the dishes as Madison entered.

"You still feeling okay, sweetie?"

"Yes."

"Your wrist didn't sting today?"

"No. I had fun riding with Uncle Ross. Except he doesn't stay on the path."

"It was so cool." Mason set the plates in place. "We had to duck away from tree branches and we saw parts of our woods we didn't know were there. You'd have hated it, Aunt Stacia."

"You're right there." She turned the burner off, drained the liquid then transferred the pot of noodles onto a hot pad in the middle of the table. "Did you see any snakes?"

"No. But a spider came after Madison."

"I'm with you Aunt Stacia." Madison shuddered. "I like the path."

"Maybe next time, you and I can stay on the path on our horses, while the boys go exploring." Stacia loved the outdoors, riding the side-by-side and horses, but she liked sure footing, head room and no critters. "Tell Grandpa the food's ready, Mason."

"Grandpa! The food's ready!" Mason shouted.

"That's not exactly what I meant. I could have done that." Stacia set the sauce and breadsticks on the table, then grabbed the salad she'd already put together along with dressing out of the fridge.

"She meant, go tell Grandpa, goofball." Madison filled the glasses with ice.

"No name-calling, Mad."

"You didn't say go." Mason plopped in his seat at the table.

"You're right, I didn't. But from now on, you'll know what I mean."

Daddy limped into the room with his weight supported on a cane.

"How's the knee?" Stacia pulled his chair out for him.

"Much better. I really don't need this cane."

"Ready to give up and have surgery?"

"I was trying to wait until the order was done."

"I'm calling tomorrow to get you an appointment. You'll probably have to wait at least a month anyway."

"Will Grandpa be like a superhero once he gets a metal knee?" Mason asked.

"Grandpa's already a superhero." Madison hugged Maverick, then took her place at the table.

"I like this one." Daddy patted her on the head.

"What about Uncle Ross?" Mason scanned the empty seat at the table. "We can't eat without him."

"He should be along any minute." Stacia checked her watch.

The doorbell buzzed.

"I'll get it." Mason darted for the living room.

Minutes later, he returned with Ross, who'd obviously gone home and cleaned up. Spicy cologne and still damp hair, looking way too handsome in his pearl-buttoned shirt and Wranglers.

"Am I late?" He took his seat between the twins, across from Stacia.

"You're right on time."

"Let's pray." Daddy bowed his head and the others followed. "Father, we thank You for this food, for our little family. Keep everyone safe and healthy from the upcoming storm. And help us to always follow Your will and glorify You in everything we do. Amen."

Amens echoed around the table as Daddy helped himself to salad and spaghetti, then passed each bowl around the table.

Forks scraped plates as everyone dug in.

"This is really good." Ross caught her gaze.

"Aunt Stacia makes her own sauce." Madison twirled her long noodles around her fork.

"Sorry about the spider." Ross grimaced.

"It's okay. Aunt Stacia said next time she'll go too and me and her will ride horses on the path."

"You should have seen it." Mason set his fork down. "We ran through a web and the spider was coming right for her." He stuck one finger up. "This is Madison and this is the spider." He made his fist with the other hand and moved it toward his finger at a fast clip.

"But Uncle Ross saved me." Madison shuddered.

"Madison screamed and Uncle Ross jumped out. He broke the web and smashed the spider." Mason stomped his foot on the floor for emphasis.

Ross winced. “But I’m the one who decided we should explore and leave the path.”

“But you fixed it.” Mason picked his fork up. “And it was the best ride I ever had. I like off the path.”

They finished the meal with constant chatter from the twins, then everyone cleaned the kitchen while Daddy went to prop his leg up in the family room.

At least she wasn’t alone with Ross in the kitchen.

“Can Uncle Ross read us a story?” Madison asked.

An automatic no danced on the tip of Stacia’s tongue.

“Please, Aunt Stacia.” Mason joined in the plea.

“Do you have time?” She caught his gaze.

“Always.”

“Okay. But go get your baths first.”

The twins hurried upstairs.

“You can go and I’ll call you when they’re ready. Baths around here can take the better part of an hour.”

“I’m in no hurry. It’s a nice night to sit out on the porch. Unless you’ve got something pressing to do.”

“That sounds nice.” Alarm bells went off in her head. *Don’t get too close.*

He ushered her ahead of him.

Outside, she claimed the porch swing, expecting him to sit in one of the chairs. But he settled beside her. She scooted over as much as she could, but it was no use. His leg rested against hers. And sent all kinds of tingles up her arms.

“This is a nice swing.”

“Thanks. Daddy made it from an old headboard.”

“I figured as much.” He took a deep breath. “I’m glad we’re getting along better.”

“Me too. For the kids’ sakes.”

“You’re starting to trust me more with them. I think we need to talk about what’s happening between us.”

"Us?" She swallowed hard.

"I'm starting to have feelings for you, Stacia. Feelings that have nothing to do with the twins." He took her hand in his.

Warm and calloused. His touch sent butterflies from her stomach to her heart. But she had to stay focused.

Memories surfaced. Of Aunt Eleanor touching Daddy's hand, leaning close.

She jerked her hand away, jumped up. "There's no us."

"Did I misunderstand?"

"Are you for real? Or are you only trying to romance me to get to the twins?"

"How can you think that?"

Playing innocent? Did he plan to woo her? Maybe even marry her so he could get custody of the twins? Or did he really care? How could she know for sure?

She couldn't. But why would he want her? Damaged goods, destined to never birth a child.

"What did your aunt do to you? How did she make you so distrustful? Was it just her or the principal too?"

"My personal life is none of your business." She jabbed a finger at him. "Just go."

"I'm not going anywhere." His jaw clenched. "Not until I read them a story like I promised. So I suggest you go hurry bath time up since we're done here."

She bolted inside, leaned against the door, hugged herself.

The only problem was, she'd been beginning to trust him. And to fall for him.

Chapter Ten

Ross hesitated outside the closed workshop doors.

After coming clean with Stacia Saturday night, he'd barely been able to focus as he'd read the twins a story. Once Stacia darted inside, he hadn't seen her again. Instead, Maverick had come to tell him the twins were story ready. Though he'd been preoccupied, spending the bonding time with his niece and nephew had been great.

He'd gone to church in Bandera yesterday, giving himself a reprieve from Stacia, then spent part of the day with the twins and Maverick.

But now with the cattle fed, he had to face her. He'd only thought things were tense and awkward between them last week. Now, he'd let his feelings for her show, but she thought it was a ploy. After all this time, after all the ways he'd worked at proving himself, she still didn't trust him.

Proving he was a brainless sap for falling for her. He'd known better. Why did he insist on banging his head against the wall? Why was he such a chump for women who couldn't trust him?

Sucking in a deep breath, Ross opened the door and strolled inside.

She didn't acknowledge him. Fine by him.

With only power tools for noise, he went to work.

Her sander died but she wouldn't look his way. "I thought you'd leave yesterday. I guess you plan to stick around until after school to say bye to the twins."

"No goodbyes and I work here."

"Not anymore. I told you to leave. You're fired."

He blew out a sigh. She'd expected him to leave Medina? A hard knot formed in his gut.

"Even if I leave, I'm still a blood relative of the twins. My parents will want to be part of their lives. We have to work something out, Stacia. You can't just send me home and ignore the situation. And besides that, you can't complete the B and B order without me. Not with Maverick laid up."

She blew out a huge sigh. "I guess you've got me there."

"Let's just finish the order. Whatever time we end up spending together with the twins, we're in this for them. We play nice, keep our distance from each other and get through this. Once the order is finished, I'll go home." To tell his folks about the twins. He dreaded that, knowing they'd be hurt that he hadn't filled them in sooner.

"Whatever you say."

"I still plan on convincing them the kids should stay with you." He stalked over to her and waited as several seconds ticked past, until she looked up. "Whether you believe it or not, I say what I mean. I don't have any ulterior motives. I'm being as straight with you as I know how to be. Okay?"

"Okay." She nodded. "We'll stick with the visitation plan we discussed with as little interaction between us as possible."

"Works for me." But his heart took a nosedive. He'd miss her. In spite of himself.

The rest of the day passed in silence, except for the buzz of the sander or the *psst* of the paint sprayer.

How could Stacia not believe he had feelings for her? Did she not realize how many times he'd wanted to kiss her? Ross had gone and done it. Fallen for Stacia Keyes in a mere matter of three weeks. And told her about it. Yet there was no getting around her distrust.

So they'd had several nice moments with the twins. She'd shown some vulnerability, revealed her deepest fears about Ron. He'd let it go to his head. Allowed himself to hope for a future. But without trust, what kind of relationship could they have? None.

Maybe it was better that she thought his profession was a ploy since she obviously didn't return his feelings. No matter what she believed, their days together were winding down. In spite of himself, he already missed her and he hadn't even left yet.

Finally when his nerves could take no more, a knock sounded from the store door. He checked his watch as Stacia turned off her spray gun. Time for the twins.

"Y'all come around back," Stacia called. "But don't come in, it's really fumy in here."

"Okay," Madison said.

Minutes passed and both kids appeared outside the open back doors.

"We have an idea," Mason announced.

"What's that?" Stacia slipped her goggles up.

"Since we don't have any homework, we want to take you to play putt-putt again." Madison grinned.

"Is that so?" Stacia smiled, for the first time all day.

"You always love it and we don't play much since we always want to swim."

"I'm game." She slipped her mask and goggles off, then shrugged out of her smock.

"Can you come too, Uncle Ross?" Mason asked. "It's more fun with four."

"I wish." Ross winced, as if he really hated it, even though he didn't. Escaping Stacia's silence for a few hours would make his day. "I'll have to stay here and work."

The door from the store opened and Maverick limped in. "I say y'all go and I can stay here and work."

"No, Daddy. You only went back to the store today. I don't want you overdoing it."

"I can sit down and paint."

"You can't even paint standing up."

Madison chuckled. "She's right, Grandpa. You make a drippy mess when you paint."

"Okay, but I can sand sitting down and I can put together coffee bars while I lean against the work table."

"I don't know." Stacia obviously didn't want him to go.

Any more than Ross did. "We'll make it some other time."

"Please." Mason resorted to begging.

"Just go for an hour." Maverick approached the worktable. "I'll do what I can without hurting myself and we're still ahead on the order anyway. An hour won't hurt. You both deserve some time off."

"Let's go." Mason and Madison echoed each other, then Mason grabbed Ross's hand while Madison grabbed Stacia's and tugged.

"Okay." Ross caved.

"I better stay here and help Grandpa." Stacia tried to beg off.

"No way." Madison tugged harder. "The whole putt-putt thing is for you."

"Go." Daddy shooed them toward the door.

"Okay. We'll take my SUV." She gave in.

"Yay." The twins jumped up and down and as usual, their voices blended together.

But it didn't sound like Stacia planned to enjoy herself.

Because of him. He'd gone and ruined the progress they'd made by admitting his feelings. Feelings she didn't believe and couldn't trust. Too bad her rebuff didn't make his feelings go away.

She grabbed her purse and they filed out of the workshop. The kids raced ahead to the vehicle. Ross was tempted to sit in the back, but he was pretty sure he couldn't maneuver around the car seat to get in, so he ended up in front.

Soon they were on the road and Mason and Madison filled the drive with chatter about what happened at school.

At the dude ranch, Ross paid the fee and collected their clubs and balls.

"I'm first." Mason scampered toward the beginning of the course, where a plywood cowboy silhouette stood near a tin cup hole.

"A gentleman always lets ladies go first." Ross did an exaggerated bow.

"Okay, you go first Madison."

Madison set her ball on the green and did a few practice swings, then sailed her ball into the hole.

Stacia was next. Her swing was awkward, but she still managed to make a hole in one.

Mason followed suit with ease as did Ross.

"We're all even." Madison wrote down their scores. "But it gets harder as you go."

She was right. Their next stop had a slight curve to the green, but they all managed to make it.

The third hole had a hill to it and Stacia missed.

"Come on, Aunt Stacia, you can do it." Madison encouraged.

"Remember I never claimed to be good at it." Stacia laughed as she missed her second try.

"Here, let me help." Ross put his hand over hers on her club.

She jerked away. "It's not a big deal. I'm just trying to have fun."

"Let him help you, Aunt Stacia." Mason pinched his nose closed with his finger and thumb. "You really stink."

"Oh do I now?"

"You really could use some lessons." Madison leaned on her club. "You like putt-putt so much. Why not let Uncle Ross teach you, so you can be good at it?"

Stacia let out a big breath. "Okay, go ahead and try."

"First thing you should do is relax." He gripped her shoulders and she stiffened more, so he let go. "Now align your feet side by side. Good." He touched her hand on the club and she flinched. "Move your grip up a little."

Standing just behind her, he covered both of her hands with his, which made her stiffen up again. "Now make sure your swing is lined up with the ball, give it a smooth tap, and follow through." He let go of her, stepped back. "Now relax. You try."

She did a shoulder roll, swung and putted. Her ball bounced, hit the hill and plunked in the gravel outside the green.

"Whoa. I didn't think you could get worse." Mason laughed.

"You definitely need more lessons, Aunt Stacia." Madison tried to contain her giggles.

"No more lessons." Stacia retrieved her ball, took two more putts to make the hole, then stepped aside so Mason could have his turn. “Just let me have fun and get through the course.”

But it was obvious she wasn’t having any.

The final shipment was set for Saturday. Whatever weather the hurricane blew at them should be cleared out by then. Then Ross would go home. And when his folks came to meet the twins, he’d try to skip it. He’d had enough of Stacia Keyes to last him a lifetime. His only choice was to get her out of his system.

Silence reined between Stacia and Ross in the workshop the next day, until she almost longed for small talk. Almost. Their close encounter at the putt-putt golf course had haunted her thoughts since.

But the twins should be home any minute and she’d escape his presence for the rest of the day. One more workday and they should be able to complete the B and B order. And then what?

“I’ve made a decision.” Ross tested the sturdiness of the coffee bar he’d just completed.

Could he read her thoughts? “And?”

“We should be able to finish the order tomorrow, right?”

“Yes.”

“Once we get everything done, I’ll help you get the delivery truck loaded and then I’m going home. To Houston. To help prepare in case the hurricane hits and tell my folks about Madison and Mason. They’ll probably want to come here to meet the twins, but I’m not coming back to Medina. Once we set up a visitation schedule, I’ll see Mason and Madison in Bandera and eventually when they come to Houston.”

“Okay.” Resignation tinged her tone. If his parents went

along with his plan and didn't take her to court, everything would be okay. Except that she'd miss Ross.

His phone rang. He hesitated, then answered. "Hey Mom."

Stacia's nerve endings pulled taut.

"Now?" His gaze caught hers. "Well, I guess it's time to tell you—I'm not there. I never made it there."

Her mind raced. Something was up, she could tell by his jerky movements.

"No. I'm with a—a friend—about an hour from Papaw's place. It's a long story. In fact, I was planning to come home in a few days and tell y'all all about it. But now—" He ran his hand through his hair. "Yeah, I'll send you the address. Okay, see you then." He ended the call.

She held her breath.

"There's an evacuation order in effect for Houston. Looks like I won't have time to go home." He slipped his phone back in his pocket. "They were planning on going to my grandparents' ranch in Hondo."

"So what address are you sending them?" She ground the words out between clenched teeth.

"Yours. They're coming here to meet my friend before they go on to Papaw's."

"What?" All the blood drained from her face.

"It's time to tell them anyway. I was going home to do just that."

"But I thought I'd have a little time." Free of him, for her nerves to settle before his parents showed up.

"I did too. But the hurricane threw everything off."

"When will they be here?"

"Tomorrow night. I'll reserve them a cabin in Bandera. And they've got some kind of surprise for me."

"Tomorrow?" she squeaked. Who cared about his surprise?

"When they get here, I'll just tell them what's going on and they can meet the twins."

A knock sounded at the store door and she checked her watch. The twins.

She took several deep breaths. "Come on in."

Mason blasted through first as usual. "Guess what happened today?"

"What?" Stacia had to fight to focus.

"Our teacher threw up. All over her desk. It was so gross." Mason grimaced.

"Mrs. Jenkins is gonna have a baby." Madison plopped her backpack in the desk chair. Stacia's eyes stung. The news of their teacher becoming a mother on top of the impending arrival of the twins' grandparents—it was all too much.

Daddy strolled into the workshop. "What's going on?"

"Can you take care of the kids for a few minutes and then help Ross in the workshop tonight?" Stacia jerked her goggles, mask and smock off, flung them on the desk and scurried toward the back door.

"I think Mason made her sick telling about our teacher throwing up," Madison said.

Out the door, Stacia bolted for the house, and up to her room. Tears streaming, she shut the door of her room and sank to the floor.

One day. She had one day to prepare for what could turn into the fight of her life. If the Lyles sued her for custody, Stacia would win. Just as Daddy had beat Aunt Eleanor's scheming tactics. And if some crazy judge ruled against her, she'd take the twins and run if she had to.

With a forecast full of storms and powerful wind gusts, the tension built to a boil as Ross completed the last coffee bar. With red-rimmed eyes and splotchy cheeks, Stacia hadn't acknowledged him all day long. Only the sounds of her paint sprayer echoed through the workshop. Would this day never end?

"Listen, my parents are coming, whether you like it or not. It won't help anything if we're not speaking or at each other's throats. Did you tell Mason and Madison they're coming?"

"No."

"Don't you think you should remedy that?" He bit back his irritation. "We're running out of time."

"Daddy and I decided not to tell them, so it won't seem like such a big deal." It was the most she'd said all day.

"Okay. However you want to play it." He sank the last screw to secure the coffee bar and tested to make sure it was sturdy. "One hundred."

"I guess I owe you my gratitude," she grudgingly admitted. "I couldn't have completed the order without you."

"You're welcome." He removed his goggles and smock. "I'll get the finished pieces loaded in the truck, then tend to the cattle early since the storm's picking up." He scanned the workshop. "You've just got the two tubs and one coffee bar left to paint. Right?"

"Yes."

He wrapped five ready-to-go coffee bars in padded sheeting and loaded them into the truck, laying them down on their sides with cardboard batting between them and the bathtubs they'd already loaded. Then he wrapped three claw-foot tubs.

"When will your dad's salvage guy be here?"

"He's stuck in San Antonio due to the storm. Let me finish painting this last piece and I'll help you."

"I don't know if that's a good idea. These things are cast iron. They weigh a ton."

"Trust me, I've loaded my share of claw-foot tubs over

the years." She sprayed the final edge of the last coffee bar, turned her sprayer off and strolled over to him. "I'll get this end."

"You sure?"

"I helped you load the ones we got from Maisy." She rolled her eyes. "Just take care of your end and I'll handle mine."

They lifted the tub, but he could tell it was a strain on her slight form. He backed his end into the trailer and they managed to set it down without mashing fingers or toes. Two more times, they repeated the process. By the time everything was loaded, she was winded.

"You okay?"

"Fine."

A knock sounded at the door and they both checked their watches. Time for school to be out already.

"Come in."

Mason and Madison entered the workroom, both wearing yellow rain slickers and rubber boots. Adorable.

"Anybody throw up today?" He ruffled Mason's hair.

"No. It was so boring." Mason groaned.

Ross chuckled, turned toward Stacia. "I'm going to round up the cattle, make sure they're all in the barnyard, and put the mamas and babies in the stalls. Once I take care of the stock, these last few pieces should be dry. I'll come back and help you wrap and get them loaded in the truck." He darted out the door as eager to escape her as she was him.

A steady rain had started and the wind picked up as he made his way to the barn. Halfway there, the bottom of the sky fell out. In a matter of minutes, his hair and clothing plastered to him. Chilled, once he made it inside the barn he shook his hair away from his face, slinging water like a wet dog.

In the supply stall, he grabbed a feed bucket, loaded it with grain and stuck a few range cubes in his pocket for the stubborn ones. He turned and ran into Stacia head on. The bucket slipped from his hand as he grabbed her shoulders to steady her.

"Sorry, I didn't know you were there."

"I came to help." Her hair clung to the sides of her face, making her appear younger, vulnerable. Scared.

Despite the tension between them, despite her determination to never trust him, he had the almost overwhelming desire to comfort her fears. She just looked so...

Kissable.

"Go on back inside, I'm fine." He let go of her, knelt to retrieve the bucket.

"If I help, we can get finished quicker and get the truck loaded, so we can get inside where it's warm and dry before your folks get here."

"Fair enough." He retrieved what grain he could from the hay-strewn floor, then scooped more from the fifty gallon drum to make up for what he'd spilled.

"I'll get the horses." She grabbed a second bucket, scooped horse feed into it and hurried out of the stall. While he poured grain into the trough down the middle of the barn galley, she filled the horses' troughs in each stall. When she finished, she placed her finger and thumb in her mouth and produced an impressively loud whistle.

Six horses straggled into the barn and he helped her secure each in their stalls.

She peered out into the distance and repeated the whistle. "Where's the sorrel and her foal?"

"They'll show up. I'll go ahead and wrangle the cows, then if they don't show, I'll go look for them." He banged on the metal bucket. Soon a trail of cattle meandered toward the barn. He counted as they entered the barn yard and when all were accounted for, he darted out into the rain and shut the gate. Scanning as far as he could see, there was no sign of the mare or her foal.

He splashed his way back to the barn, soaked through and mud caked. "I don't see them. You go on to the house, tend to the twins, and I'll go look for them. When I get back, we'll finish loading the truck."

"I shouldn't have let them out this morning." She hugged herself. "I knew this weather was coming."

"It's not your fault. It hit a little sooner than the weatherman said it would. And I'm sure they're fine. They probably sought shelter in the woods. I'll find them."

"Be careful."

"I will." He opened the stall where she'd just secured his horse, put the saddle and bit in place in record time, and rode out into the deluge.

Was she worried about him? Nah, just the mare and the foal. Any worries she cast his way were for the twins' sake. Stacia Keyes couldn't wait to see his taillights. And he'd be happy to oblige her. As soon as the evacuation was over and the B and B shipment was safely on its way, he was out of there. With no looking back.

Chapter Eleven

With Wednesday night Bible study canceled due to the storm, the twins were already fed and bathed. Daddy was upstairs readying them for bed while Stacia paced the kitchen floor. Ross should be back by now, with the mare and foal safely in the barn.

His parents were due to roll up any minute. With severe thunderstorm warnings and tornado watches spawned from the hurricane, the wind howled outside and rain slammed against the window, and they still had to finish loading the truck.

At least it was almost the twins' bedtime. Maybe meeting their grandparents could be put off until tomorrow.

Small feet scurried down the stairs. Mason jumped over the last three steps and landed at the bottom. Madison followed, but didn't do any jumping.

"Why aren't y'all in bed?" She tapped Mason's nose.

"We're worried about Uncle Ross and Stockings and Rust," he whined.

"A little rain won't hurt him or the horses."

"But Rust is just a baby." Madison yawned.

Obviously two tired twins.

"Let's get y'all in bed and they'll all be here in the

morning when everybody wakes up." Along with Ross's parents.

A knock sounded at the door. Please let it be Ross and not his folks.

The twins bolted for it and Mason opened the door.

It wasn't Ross. An older couple and a man with way-too-long hair stood on the porch. Relatively dry, folding up two umbrellas. The younger man seemed familiar.

"Well, hello," the woman said. "I'm not sure we're at the right place. We're looking for Ross Lyles."

"This is the right place." She forced the words, then offered her hand. "I'm Stacia Keyes."

The younger man gasped as his eyes widened.

And Stacia figured out where she'd seen him.

In court. Ronny Outrageous.

"I just need to get these two to bed." She nabbed each of the twins' hands and practically dragged them toward the stairs. "Come on in. I'll be right back."

"But we wanna see who they are," Mason grumbled.

"Just some friends of Ross's. You can meet them in the morning."

"But why not now?"

"Because it's past your bedtime and you're both cranky."

"Stop arguing, Mason. You're gonna get us in trouble," Madison said.

Thankfully, the two fell into silence the rest of the way up the stairs. How could Ross do this to her? How long had he had it planned for his brother to ambush her? He must want the twins back. Why else would he be here? Yes, Calli had made her their legal guardian, but Stacia had seen too many children ripped away from loved ones in the headlines.

Daddy met them on the landing. "Was that Ross I heard come in?"

"No. His guests are here. Three of them." She did a head nod toward the kids.

But Daddy squinted, obviously not picking up on her meaning. "You get these two in bed and I'll go tend to them."

Inside the twins' room, she tucked them both in, but the cozy room with its horse decor failed to soothe her. Somehow, she managed to read them *Where the Wild Things Are*, though she was completely distracted and both kids were dozing before she reached the end.

She quietly left the room and headed down the stairs. Voices. Ross and his mom.

"It just worries me that you're dating a woman with twins, sweetheart. That's a lot to take on."

Huh? Stacia wasn't one to eavesdrop, but avoiding the awkward conversation forced her to take a seat on the step.

"You don't understand, Mom. She's not my girlfriend. But, I'll admit, if things were different, she might be."

But Ross's attempts to woo her would fail. He was still up to something. And his brother was obviously in on it. But why had he seemed shocked when she'd told them her name?

"Listen, we need to talk, but it'll have to wait until tomorrow. Right now, I have a mare and her new foal I have to find. I just came back to make sure y'all made it in okay."

"I'll help you, son," his dad said. "Karen, you and Ron go on to the cabin in Bandera and Ross can bring me there after we find the horses."

Stacia should protest. She could go out and search with Ross. But the most important thing at the moment was to get Ron out of her house.

"It's a horse." Ron snickered. "Y'all are going out in a deluge over a horse?"

"A mare with a newborn foal," Ross snapped. "With flash flood warnings. Yes I'm going after it. But you really don't have to go, Dad."

"Nonsense, I grew up braving weather like this over livestock," Ross's dad said. "Maybe we should have raised you boys on a ranch, so Ron here would know what's important."

"I'll pass."

"All right," Ross's mom cut in. "Ron's crankier than Ross's girl's twins. Let's go to the cabin."

"She's not my girl," Ross protested. "But I wish she could be."

Stacia rolled her eyes.

"Can we just go already?" Ron moaned.

"Come on." Ross's mom laughed. "It's like having a toddler when he gets tired."

Ron apparently wanted to leave as badly as Stacia wanted him to. So what was going on? Had he changed his mind about wanting the twins, but he hadn't realized Ross had been working for Stacia?

"Here we are, three sweet teas." Daddy had apparently come back into the room.

"Oh Maverick." Ross's mom's tone was apologetic. "I'm afraid we'll have to take a rain check. Ron and I are headed to the cabin and Ross and Sam are going back out to look for the mare. We should have waited until morning and not bothered you so late."

"Stacia and I are night owls," Daddy said. "You go on with your family, Sam. I can go with Ross."

"Oh, no you don't." Ross's tone left no room for argument. "You just got mobile again with that knee. Dad and I will find her."

"I appreciate it." Thankfully, Daddy gave in.

"I can at least mop up the puddle Ross made and help with the towels," Ross's mom offered.

"It's not a big deal, Karen. I'll get it."

"We'll see you tomorrow, Maverick," Ross's mom said, and the door shut behind them.

Stacia's breathing relaxed. Ron was gone. At least for now. It sounded as if Ross and his dad had left too. She stood, took a few deep breaths to steady her nerves and continued down the stairs.

Daddy stood in the foyer, staring at the door, his shoulders slumped. A puddle and wadded towels lay on the tile.

"Are we alone?" she asked.

He whirled to face her. "For the time being. What did they bring him for?"

"All I can figure is he's changed his mind about the twins."

"Over my dead body." Daddy stiffened.

"Mine too." She laid her head against Daddy's shoulder.

Ross had found rain ponchos in the barn, and Mom had insisted he change clothes before he went out again. At least their upper bodies weren't soaked through as they rode into the night.

The beam of their flashlights cut through the downpour, but so far there was no sign of the mare or her foal. If only she were a pale palomino instead of a russet-colored sorrel. Maybe the white blaze on her face or socked feet would be detectable in the darkness.

"Why didn't you tell us all of this was about a girl?"

"It's not what you think, Dad. I'll explain everything later."

"I don't know why it wouldn't be about the girl. She's

a looker. I didn't get to talk to her, but if she's half as nice as her dad, she must be something."

"Trust me Dad, this isn't about Stacia."

"Your mom's worried about you taking on twins, but I think you're man enough for the job. The only thing is, you'll be taking on some other man's kids. Is the father in the picture?"

"Dad. Please. It's not like that. Can we just concentrate on the horse for now?"

"Sure."

"I'm sorry, Dad. I'm just chilled." And bone-tired. "I need to find the mare and I'm worried about the foal, and then I still have to load the truck."

"What truck?"

"Stacia and her dad have a repurposing business. There's a coffee bar and a couple of claw-foot tubs in the barn that need to be secured in the delivery truck in case the barn gets damaged. Which is doubtful, but just in case."

"If it's not about the girl, why are you so concerned about her business?"

"I've been working here. Helping with a big order for a chain of bed-and-breakfasts."

"Why? Did you know Stacia before you came here?"

"Later, Dad." He caught a glimpse of something white in the beam of his flashlight. "I think I see her over by the pond." Ross blew a shrill whistle.

A whinny came from the darkness.

"Hey girl, where's your baby?" Ross used his soothing voice, but it was probably lost in the wind and downpour.

As they neared, the beam of their flashlights revealed the nervous mare focused on the pond. Surely her foal hadn't drowned.

They pulled their horses up close to her and dismounted.

"It's me girl." Ross patted her flank. "We're here to help." He shined his flashlight into the pond. The foal was in the edge of the pond, head far above water, but obviously cold and exhausted. "I think he's stuck."

"Loop this around your waist, so you don't get stuck too." Dad threw him his rope and secured the other end to his saddle horn.

Ross pulled the lasso down over his shoulders and tightened it around his waist. "Hey Rust. I'm coming to help you boy."

The mare shuffled her feet, whinnied.

"It's okay girl, we'll get him home." Ross's boots sucked into the wet mud as he neared the pond. No wonder the foal got stuck. "Hey guy, let me help you out of there."

He stroked the foal's face, then wrapped his arms around the shivering middle. With a good tug, he pulled the foal's hooves free.

"There we go. We'll all be warm in no time now." Dad dismounted and helped Ross get the foal up on his horse.

At least the exhausted baby was too tired to struggle. Minutes later, they were riding back to the barn with the mud-caked foal lying across Ross's lap.

"I'm so glad we found him," Dad said. "He definitely wouldn't have lasted until morning. We'd have found him drowned."

"Thanks for helping. It was a lot easier to get him with your help. And he's too exhausted to walk."

"Kind of like old times, when you were a kid, helping me and your papaw on his ranch. Once we get him settled, I'll help you load the truck too."

"I'm glad you're here, Dad." And Ross meant it from the bottom of his heart.

Things would get tough over the next few days. His folks would likely be upset that Ron never told them about the twins. That Ross had known over the last month and kept it from them. But the truth needed to come out. His parents had been robbed of being grandparents. It was high time they knew the truth.

Once they made it back to the barn, they settled the mare and foal in their stall with lots of fresh hay for warmth and put out extra oats for sustenance. The mare contently licked her offspring and he was starting to respond.

"He'll be fine." Dad patted Ross's shoulder. "Ready to load that truck?"

"You can go on to the workshop through those big double doors. I'll run to the house, let them know we found them and be right back." Ross trotted toward the house, splashing as he went. Careful not to bust it on the wet steps, he made his way up on the porch and knocked.

Stacia opened it quick, as if she'd been waiting on the other side.

"We found them. They're okay. The foal was stuck in the mud at the edge of the pond."

"Oh the poor baby. Are you sure he's okay?"

"He's dazed, cold and exhausted from trying to get out. But we gave them plenty of food and hay. Stockings was cleaning him up and he was moving around, so he should be fine by morning."

"Thank you. For finding them."

"Dad and I will finish loading the truck and get it secured, then I'll check on him again before I head to the cabin with them."

"Do they know about Mason and Madison?"

"Not yet."

"Why is Ron here?"

"Apparently he was my surprise. But he had no idea I was here with you." He took his hat off long enough to slick his hair back under it. "I'll hash it out with Ron tonight. Find out what his plans are. I can almost promise you he has no interest in the twins."

Distrust shone in her eyes. "He saw them. For the first time."

"If I know my brother, it won't make any difference."

"I hope you're telling me the truth."

"That's all I've done since I've known you, Stacia." His words came out sharp. "I can't help it if you don't trust me."

"Will you tell your parents tonight?"

"Hey," Dad's voice came from a few yards away. "The workshop is locked."

"Sorry Dad." He turned away from her, unable to stand the torture of looking at her a minute longer. "I've got the key."

"Thank you so much for helping with the horses and for agreeing to load the truck, Mr. Lyles."

"Please, call me Sam. And it was my pleasure. It was kind of nice to do ranch work again. Thank you for letting us come to visit Ross. I look forward to getting to know you and your twins better."

"Me too."

Ross forced himself to look her way. A silent agreement passed between them. Tomorrow.

"Let's go, Dad. It's getting late." He turned away from her and darted toward the workshop with Dad following.

Every muscle he owned ached. From manhandling the foal out of the mud and onto his horse, from loading the claw-foot tubs earlier. And he still had more to load. But more than his muscles, his heart hurt. No matter what he did, no matter what he said, Stacia would never trust him.

* * *

Bone-tired, Ross left his mucky boots on the porch and followed his Dad into the Bandera rental cabin.

"You found them?" Mom started to greet them with a hug, but stopped to scan their dripping attire and scurried to the adjoining bathroom. "I'll get towels."

Ron sprawled on one of the beds, barely looking away from his phone to acknowledge them.

"We did find them." Dad dried off, then removed his jacket and explained about the foal.

"Will he be okay?"

"He's warm in a stall with his mom now." Ross dried off enough to earn a hug from Mom. He clasped her tight against his chest, feeling a bit like the foal. The familiar smell of her Avon perfume soothed his soul. "I've missed y'all."

A lump formed in his throat with all he wanted to tell them. But Stacia needed to be there when the truth came out. She'd earned that right by raising the twins thus far.

"You too. So what's the mystery? If Stacia isn't your girlfriend, why are you here?"

"About that, Stacia and I will explain everything tomorrow. Tonight, I need to talk to Ron for a minute."

Ron looked up from his phone.

Mom chuckled. "Well, I'd love to give you boys some privacy, but the only place your father and I can go is in the bathroom and it's pretty tight quarters."

"In my truck." He shot Ron a look, daring him to argue.

"Let's go."

"It's late, so after we talk, I'll shove off. But I'll see y'all in the morning. Come to the ranch about ten or so."

"We'll be there." Dad's eyes said he wanted to ask more questions, but he didn't.

Ross ushered Ron out and to his truck. Inside the cab,

he gripped the steering wheel, focused on the sheet of rain crashing into the windshield.

"Why are you here? With her?" Ron slammed the passenger's door.

"I wanted to see my niece and nephew. To make sure they're all right."

"They looked fine to me. Have you been here the entire time?"

"Seeing them did nothing to you, did it?"

"They're kids. You know that's not my thing."

"I don't understand you." Ross gripped the steering wheel even harder. "From the moment you told me about them, I had to see them. And once I did, they melted my heart. I can't imagine my life without Mason and Madison in it."

"So that's what she named them. I'd forgotten. Clever for twins." Ron stretched his back, something he'd done often since his accident. "Look, I told you about them, in a weak moment when I thought I might die. I didn't mean for you to go all uncle on me. I guess you plan on telling Mom and Dad."

"Of course I do." Ross let out an exasperated sigh. "They're grandparents, don't you think they'd like to know that."

"I guess." Ron shrugged.

"I was about to head home to tell them, when they called and said they were being evacuated. Since they're here, Stacia and I will tell them together. I don't guess you'd like to be there."

"Not at all. I was planning to take off and this whole hurricane thing put a wrench in my plans. All I want to do is get back on the road and salvage what's left of my career."

"I'm not surprised."

"Enough of the browbeating, big brother. I'm not a paragon of virtue like you and I never will be. So get over it already."

"Trust me, I am."

"I'm supposed to be in a treatment center right now."

"Well, that's a good plan."

"If I have to stay in this tiny cabin with the folks one more minute, I'll go crazy. I'm thinking I need to take off tonight."

"Um, in case you haven't noticed, there's a hurricane-scale storm out there."

"It's letting up."

Ross peered through the windshield. He could see more clearly and the rain wasn't pounding anymore.

"You could take me to a center in San Antonio."

"Tomorrow."

"Tonight. I don't know, all this drama, it's making me antsy."

For the first time in years, Ron was clean and Ross didn't need a reversal. "What about Mom and Dad?"

"You can tell them where I went when you get back."

"You can tell them now."

"Seriously?"

"If you go in and tell them, right now, I'll take you. Tonight."

Ron rolled his eyes, but opened the truck door and got out.

Ross followed.

"What?" Ron splayed his hands. "You don't trust me?"

"No, brother. I'm afraid I don't." He checked his watch, almost midnight. "Hurry up with it, we're getting soaked again and I'd like to go to bed sometime tonight."

They splashed their way back to the cabin.

Ross didn't trust his brother just as surely as Stacia had no faith in him. But the difference was, Ron had given him plenty of reason for distrust, while Ross hadn't given Stacia any.

Chapter Twelve

Though it was Thursday, school was out due to flooded roads on the bus route and an enormous fallen tree that damaged the lunchroom. Stacia had left the twins to sleep in with Daddy. With the B and B order complete and loaded, she was at loose ends and it wasn't time to open the store yet. She stepped outside, saw Ross's truck and vaulted toward the barn.

The rain had stopped during the night, but the ground was soaked, sucking at her boots with each step.

The cattle and horses stood contentedly at their troughs and she found Ross in the stall with Stockings and Rust. The foal was up and nursing.

"He looks great, doesn't he?" Ross didn't turn to face her. "If you could have seen him last night, you'd be impressed with his progress."

"I'm really glad you found them. So, did you tell your folks yet?"

"No, I told them to come to the store at ten. I figure we can break the news together."

She drew in a big breath, closed her eyes. "What about Ron?"

"He left last night. Being here was too much for him."

Anger edged his tone. "I took him to a treatment center in San Antonio."

"In the storm? When did you get back?"

"It let up a little by the time we left. I got back about two a.m."

"You must be exhausted. We could put off—"

"No we can't." He whirled around to face her. "It's been put off long enough."

"Okay. But school's out, so the kids are still in bed. We'll have to have our discussion in the workshop."

"I figured as much. That's why I told them to come to the store."

"Have they heard anything about their house or the business yet?"

"No. They probably won't know until they head home. Unless some of their neighbors get there before they do."

"That would drive me crazy, not knowing if I still had a house or not." But not as bad as how she felt right now. Waiting for his folks to show up. They'd probably be angry she never tried to find them.

"I guess they're used to it."

An engine sounded, the crunch of gravel.

"I think they're here." He finally came out of the stall, ambled through the galley around the cows and peered toward the drive. "Yep, that's them."

She checked her watch. "It's nine fifteen."

"I guess they're eager. They were wanting to know what was going on last night. The only way I was able to put them off was leaving and staying gone so late." He adjusted his hat, turned in her direction. "You ready?"

"No. They'll probably be really mad."

"Probably. But they're good folks. They'll forgive and the important thing to them will be Mason and Madison."

So important they'd want custody?

"Come on." He reached a hand toward her.

She frowned at his outstretched fingers.

"I figure we're in this together."

Forcing her feet to move, she took his hand simply because she wasn't sure her noodle legs would hold up without his support. They rounded the barn and as they neared the store, his parents got out of their car.

"Sorry we're early." Ross's mom glanced at their linked hands. "We were just so anxious to know what's going on. Are you sure Ron is okay?"

"I dropped him at the treatment center. He was settling in when I left."

"Your mother worried all night about y'all being out in the storm."

"I'm sorry, Mom. It was so late, I didn't want to call and wake you."

Stacia felt sorry for the woman. One son was a mess and in treatment and now her world was about to be shaken with the discovery of five-year-old grandchildren.

"I apologize, Stacia." His mom smiled. "We barely met last night and we've dragged you into our family drama."

"No need to apologize, Mrs. Lyles."

"Please, call me Karen." So friendly and warm. Her eyes the same shade as her sons'. White hair cut in an attractive face-framing short style and large trendy glasses completed her look.

"Let's go inside." Ross gestured toward the store.

Stacia unlocked the front door and stepped aside so his parents could enter first.

"Oh my, this place is really something." Sam scanned the space. "It reminds me of that TV show, where they salvage old buildings."

"Daddy owns a salvage business and that is where we get a lot of our pieces. But he started about ten years earlier than those guys on TV and he never got his own show."

"Everything's so unique." Karen spun a circle. "Everywhere I look, I want to explore."

"Let's talk first." Ross opened the door to the workshop. "You'll have plenty of time for exploring."

"I'm not sure how much longer we'll stay, son." Sam ushered his wife ahead. "We still haven't made it to your grandfather's and we'll want to get home soon and see what's left."

"I think after you hear what we have to say, you'll decide to stay."

Sam and Karen caught each other's gaze as they stepped inside the workshop.

"You're kind of worrying us," Sam admitted.

"It's good news, mostly." Ross gave his parents a tight smile.

"Please, have a seat." Stacia pulled four office-style chairs into the center of the room, forming a trapezoid with two close together for his parents and two farther apart. "Excuse the dust and debris. This is where we sand, build and paint."

His parents sat side by side while Ross and Stacia claimed the two chairs facing them.

"The suspense is killing us, just spit it out, son." Sam clasped his wife's hand.

"Okay. Y'all are grandparents."

"What?" Karen glanced from Ross to Stacia. "I don't understand. Are you preg—"

"No!" Stacia cut her off.

"The twins y'all saw last night." Ross drew in a deep breath. "They're your grandchildren."

"So you and Stacia had a relationship in the past?" Sam ventured.

"No!" Stacia shook her head.

"We only met a few weeks ago," Ross clarified. "Ron is their father."

"So Stacia and Ron—"

"No!" Stacia interrupted again. "Ron and my sister."

"Twins. Our grandchildren?" Karen shook her head as if to clear it.

"Where is their mother, your sister?" Sam asked.

"She died three years ago and left custody to me."

"And Ron?" Sam's gaze fell to the concrete floor. "Does he know about them?"

"Yes."

"Let me guess, he's had nothing to do with them."

"He signed his rights over to Stacia's sister and then Stacia." Ross summed up Ron's disinterest for them. "He'd never even seen them until y'all showed up here last night."

"How old are they?" Karen asked.

"Five."

"We've missed out on so much." Her shoulders slumped. "What are their names?"

"Mason and Madison. I'm sorry you're just now finding out." Stacia's voice trembled.

"Someone should have told us all right." Sam stood and paced the floor. "But it should have been Ron."

"Or Ross." Karen pinned him with a look. "Why didn't you tell us?"

"I didn't know. Not until after Ron's accident. I spent the night at the hospital with him after his back surgery. He was in so much pain he thought he might die and confessed to fathering twins and giving them away. I got Stacia's name out of him and came here to see the twins and make sure they're all right."

"So you've been here since you left? Getting to know

our grandchildren." Sam paced faster. "But no one thought to invite us to meet them."

"My intention when I came was to make sure Stacia was a suitable guardian. Once I checked things out, I planned to tell y'all. But Stacia had a big order for a B and B, I needed to stay here until we finished it, and I didn't want to tell you over the phone. I was planning to head home when you called and told me about the evacuation order."

"Ron told us he didn't have any family." Stacia's voice cracked. "I can assure you both, I'm a suitable guardian."

"Mom, Dad, I promise you, Stacia and her father love the kids and the kids love them. They're happy and healthy. And Stacia and her dad are willing to let us be a part of their lives."

"Y'all are welcome to stay as long as you want and spend as much time with Madison and Mason as you like." She could only hope she didn't sound as desperate as she felt. "We hope you'll visit often. And maybe on school holidays or in the summer, they can visit y'all in Houston."

Please don't ask for more. Please don't take them.

"I just can't believe this. We should have known about this, before they were born." Sam kept up his pacing.

"Getting angry doesn't help anything." Karen stood, cut her husband off and grasped his hands. "We have two adorable redheaded grandchildren. We're wasting time talking and pacing, when we could be meeting them."

Sam blew out a big breath, just the way Stacia had seen Ross do countless times.

"You're right." Sam hugged his wife. "As usual. When can we meet our grandchildren?"

"There's no time like the present." Ross looked her way.

"They should be awake by now." Stacia tried to put some enthusiasm in her response. "Let's go to the house."

"I'm sorry for barging in on you like this, Stacia." Karen's tone echoed her apology. "We had no idea of the situation when we decided to invite ourselves here. When Ross said he was with a friend, we assumed you were his girlfriend and wanted to meet you."

"It's fine." *Just don't try to take them and everything will be fine.*

She stood, legs still noodly, and led the way to the house.

Inside, chatter came from the kitchen as Ross's parents hesitated in the foyer.

"Come on in. Sounds like Daddy's cooking breakfast. Are y'all hungry?" Thankfully her voice held up and she didn't sound as jittery as she felt. She hoped.

"I couldn't eat a thing." Karen pressed a hand to her midriff. "My stomach is doing acrobatics."

"They're great kids," Ross said. "They'll love y'all."

"I hope so." Karen smoothed her hands down each side of her slacks.

"This way." Stacia led the way to the kitchen.

In the kitchen, Daddy was flipping pancakes and catching them in the skillet as the twins giggled. Even though they'd seen his antics countless times. He noticed the Lyleses and promptly dropped a pancake for the first time Stacia could ever remember.

"Grandpa, you missed it." Mason frowned. "You never miss it."

"I think we distracted him." Ross took the blame. "Y'all have company."

"Uncle Ross." Mason scampered over to hug his new favorite person.

Maybe he'd move down the list once the twins met their other grandparents. But that would put Stacia way down the roll.

"We don't have school for the rest of the week." Madison gave him a high five and then got her hug. "I like school. But I like sleeping in and eating pancakes too. It's like we'll have a really long weekend."

"You're right."

"Y'all were here last night." Mason stared at Sam and Karen.

"You're right. We were."

"With that long-haired guy. Where's he?"

Stacia held her breath. They'd forgotten to discuss Ron with his parents.

"He needed help, so we got him some," Ross said. "He left last night."

She started breathing again.

"I want y'all to meet my parents."

Since Madison was fascinated with relatives, Stacia knew she'd put it together and saw the light in the child's eyes when she did.

"So you're our grandparents?"

"You're a very bright girl." Karen stepped farther into the room.

"Her report card is always better than mine." Mason peered at them. "If y'all are our grandparents, then you know our dad."

Stacia's heart almost leaped out of her chest. "The twins know about their dad's job and how it's so important he doesn't get to see them."

"That's right." Karen's eyes turned glossy. "I'm sorry about that. But your grandfather and I are here. And we want to spend lots of time with you both."

"Did you just find out about us, like Uncle Ross?" Madison asked.

"Yes." Sam leaned against the countertop. "But now that we know, you'll be seeing a lot of us."

"Yay!" The twins' voices blended as they often did.

"Would you like some pancakes?" Daddy asked. "I promise not to drop them on the floor."

"I can't remember the last time I had pancakes." Karen's eyes closed in an obvious effort to pull her emotions together. "I hate to put you to the trouble though."

"No trouble." Daddy poured more batter into his skillet. "Have a seat and they'll be coming right up."

Karen and Sam claimed the two chairs facing the twins.

"We like peanut butter and syrup on our pancakes." Mason traced his finger through a trail of salt he'd probably poured on the table. "What do you like on yours?"

"Usually just syrup. But we may have to try it your way." Sam grinned.

And just like that, Mason and Madison wrapped two more adults around their little fingers. Stacia just prayed they'd be content with visits.

She busied herself getting drinks and helping Daddy multitask, while trying to ignore the bonding going on.

"All right, here we go." Daddy handed her a plate piled with pancakes as he carried the scrambled eggs to the table.

Everyone claimed their seats, with Ross by his parents and Stacia flanked by the twins across from him. Daddy said a prayer, but Stacia didn't hear any of it.

"So are y'all gonna live here, like Uncle Ross?" Mason talked around his mouthful of pancakes.

"No talking with food in your mouth," Stacia reminded him.

"Sorry."

Karen chuckled. "We're just visiting on our way to see my parents in Hondo."

"So they'd be our—" Madison paused to think "—great-grandparents, right?"

"That's right, and they'll be tickled to hear all about the two of you." Karen beamed.

If there was any anger or scheming in her, she certainly didn't show it.

"Can we go with you to meet them?" Mason asked.

"What have we told you about inviting yourself places, boy?" Daddy's voice turned gruff.

But Stacia wasn't sure if it was because he was upset with Mason or the thought of the twins traveling with Sam and Karen. Her stomach churned and she set her fork down.

"Your grandfather is right." Sam sipped his coffee. "You shouldn't invite yourself places. But in this case, we'd love for you to go."

"I don't know—" Stacia tried to think of a reasonable excuse, but her brain spun.

"You could come too." Ross threw her a lifeline. "You know Nanny."

"You do?" Karen shot her a confused frown.

"I've bought items from Myrna several times. I love her store."

"What a small world. Please join us. You too, Maverick."

"When were y'all planning to head out?" Daddy forked a mouthful of pancakes.

"Saturday?" Karen and Sam's voices blended together.

"That won't work." Thankfully. "I'd love to see Myrna, but we've had this big order at the store and I have to make sure everything gets shipped that morning. And our part-time employees have been pulling double shifts so we could complete the order. I told them they could have Saturday off as a reward. It's always our busiest day, so we'll have to both be here to run the store."

"But we could still go." Madison glanced from Daddy to Stacia. "Who'll keep us if y'all are both at the store?"

"You can stay at the store with us."

"That's sooooo boring." Mason rolled his eyes.

"No eye rolling." She wagged a finger at him.

"We'd love to take the children with us. My folks would love it." Karen closed her eyes as if savoring the idea. "It's only an hour away. We could leave in the morning and be back by suppertime."

"Pleeeeeaaaaase!" the twins begged.

"Now stop that." Daddy checked his watch. "Speaking of the store, I better get to it."

"I'll go." Stacia pushed her plate away and stood. "I'll handle things there while you entertain our guests."

"If you both need to go, we'll be fine on our own." Karen started picking up plates. "These two will be plenty of entertainment."

"I can handle it. Thursdays aren't usually very busy." More than anything, Stacia wanted Daddy to stay and supervise.

"I'll clean up." Daddy tried to shoo Karen away from the table.

"But what about Saturday?" Madison pressed.

"We'll think about it." But right now, she needed to escape. To get away from the twins longing to meet even more family members, away from Ross, away from the threat of losing Mason and Madison.

Finished with the cattle, Ross hurried toward his apartment as the sun set. He'd enjoyed two days spent with his folks, the twins and Maverick. Yesterday, they'd hung around the ranch. Today, they'd taken the kids to the dude ranch in Bandera with Maverick.

Though Stacia worked the store both days, she'd been

overly generous with letting them spend time with the twins. As if she thought she could ward off her imagined custody battle by letting his folks practically live at the ranch.

But truth be told, he'd missed her. How had she done it, wound herself into his heart, despite all his efforts of keeping her from it?

Inside, his parents waited for him.

"Hey. We're just breaking and entering." Mom chuckled. "Actually Maverick gave us a key. We're all supposed to go to Bandera for supper, so we thought we'd give them a break from us for a bit until time to go."

The first time they'd been alone since his parents had arrived. "I'm really sorry I didn't tell y'all about the kids."

"It wasn't really your place." Dad's tone was harsher than usual, a testament to how much Ron had hurt him. Hurt all of them.

"Your brother should have told us." Mom held her hands up as if warding off argument. "But it doesn't matter. We're here now and we'll have years to make up for lost time with our adorable grandchildren."

"Are y'all okay with them staying with Stacia?"

"Of course." Dad set his hat on the dresser. "Houston isn't that far. We can visit back and forth."

"I told her that, but she's afraid y'all will sue her for custody."

"Oh no, we'd never do that." Mom shook her head. "I mean unless they were being neglected or mistreated. But they're obviously happy and this is their home."

"Maybe she'll believe it if y'all tell her."

"We most certainly will."

"You really like her, don't you?" Dad raised an eyebrow.

"It doesn't matter."

"You don't think she likes you?" Mom scrutinized him. "I think you're wrong. There's something in the way she looks at you."

"She doesn't trust me. I told her how I felt and she thought I was using her to get custody of the twins."

"Well maybe once we tell her she can keep the kids, she'll settle down and see the real you." Mom patted his arm.

"Thanks." Not likely. And he couldn't go through the whole distrustful relationship again. Once was enough. "Have I got time to clean up?"

Dad checked his watch. "Twenty minutes."

Ross took a quick shower and as he towel dried his hair after dressing, a knock sounded at the apartment door. When he stepped out of the bathroom, Stacia was there, just inside the open door as if she might need a hasty escape.

All the oxygen drained out of him at her presence.

"We're still on for supper, right?" Mom asked.

"Our treat." Dad tried to sweeten the pot.

"Yes. Daddy will be here with the kids soon. I wanted to come over a bit early. To ask—to beg." Her eyes turned glossy. "Please don't take them away from us. You can visit anytime you want. I realize Ron may change his mind on our custody arrangement, since he saw them, but I can't lose them."

"Oh honey." Mom hugged her. "We're not in the business of uprooting children."

"If you can't trust me on anything else," Ross caught her gaze over Mom's shoulder, "trust me on this. Though it pains me to say it, Ron has no interest."

"Look at everybody getting along." Maverick stepped inside the open door. "I've got two hungry Keyes children raring to go."

Maybe getting to know his parents a bit tonight would appease her. If his folks could work out a visitation schedule, then after the day trip to Hondo, he and his parents could go back to Houston. Then deal with whatever damage there was and he could leave Stacia behind for good.

Maybe then he could repair the damage she'd done to his heart.

"Uncle Ross, your hair's all flippy." Madison giggled.

"That's cause it's wet, munchkin. We ready?" He scanned all the faces, but his gaze locked with Stacia's.

"We can wait for you to dry your hair," Mom said.

"I'm fine. Let's go."

"Can we all ride together?" Mason was obviously enthralled with his new grandparents. "We can all fit in Aunt Stacia's SUV."

Her mouth tightened, but she didn't protest.

The gathering flowed out of the apartment and loaded in the vehicle.

The fifteen-minute drive was filled with chatter from the twins as usual. Upon arriving, Stacia was able to park close.

As they stepped inside the OST, his dad looked around. "What's the name of this place?"

"The Old Spanish Trail, OST for short." Stacia gave the hostess a head count.

"Could we get a table in the John Wayne room?" The side room decorated with the Duke memorabilia was a bit more private and less noisy the times Ross had stopped in over the last month.

"Of course. Right this way."

"Isn't it awesome?" Mason pointed out the covered wagon salad bar, the saddle barstool seating and the enormous trophy elk on the wall that servers had to duck underneath.

"They don't serve alcohol here." Stacia smiled, obviously on hyper alert trying to prove she was a suitable guardian for the twins. "The bar is just for food."

Once they were seated, they gave their drink orders and checked out the menu. When their drinks arrived, the server took their food orders and left them alone.

"Thank you for making us feel so welcome." Mom patted Stacia's hand. "We'll probably head back to Houston Sunday morning."

Stacia paled. "So soon?"

Huh? Ross expected her to be glad.

"We need to check on our house and the store. But we should be able to come back in two weeks, if that's okay with you."

"Two weeks?" Her voice cracked. "The kids have school."

"Yes. If it's not too much, we'd like to come and visit Mason and Madison every other weekend."

"Visit them, here?" Some color returned to her face.

"Well, yes. This is where they live. Eventually, we might want them to come visit us, maybe in the summer. But for weekend visits, it'll be easier if we just come here. We'll try not to crowd you or be a nuisance."

Stacia clutched a hand to her heart. "That sounds fine."

She must have thought they planned to take the twins with them for two weeks.

"Wonderful. Now that we have things settled, have you decided about tomorrow?"

She glanced at Ross, then the hopeful faces of their mutual niece and nephew. "I think they'd enjoy visiting more grandparents."

"Yay!" the twins echoed one another.

"You're the best, Aunt Stacia." Mason smacked her a high five across the table.

"Thank you." Mom gave Stacia's hand a quick squeeze. "And Mason is right, you kids are very blessed to have Stacia for an aunt."

The tension eased and she seemed to relax as their food arrived.

Could Mom be right? If Stacia could get it settled in her heart that the twins were hers, could she see him in a new light? Dare he hope?

This had to be the longest day in history. Stacia had seen the twins off this morning, but it seemed like days ago. The store had kept her busy with getting the B and B shipment off and a constant flow of customers. But she'd been unable to focus and as the workday ended, she was anxious for their return.

Thankfully, the Lyleses seemed content with the twins living with her. Eventually, she'd have to deal with the twins going to Houston for visits during school holidays. She dreaded dragging them back and forth for road trips and if she took them or Ross picked them up, they'd have to see each other.

Tying her to him and his fake feelings forever.

She checked her watch. Shouldn't they be back by now? Had she been too trusting? Her hands shook.

"Relax." Daddy shot her a wink. "Ron's out of the picture. Karen and Sam are content with visits. The twins are probably having the time of their lives."

"I hope so. I really do. But I was expecting them back by now."

"They're meeting their great-grandparents for the first time. That's not something you can rush."

"I guess you're right."

"Sweetheart, the Lyles family aren't scheming, manipulative or obsessed like your aunt was."

"I hope you're right."

"I am. Why don't you go take a walk? You're wound tighter than a roll of barbed wire."

It was tempting to let the chatter of birds and the fresh air soothe her fried nerves.

"Go on. I'll close up."

"Okay." She tried to give him a reassuring smile, but didn't quite pull it off.

Outside, the sun shone bright, mid-eighties with a slight breeze. Autumn wildflowers lined the familiar path to the river. But her heart was too troubled to really appreciate it. Birds lent their voices, but peace refused to come.

By the time she made it to the river, she was ready to turn back and go home. Instead, she sat on her favorite rock near the shallow crossing and tried to let the trickle of the water wash away her worries.

"Please let them be all right Lord. Bring Madison and Mason home to me." Tears came but no more words would. He was listening. She could feel God's presence and He knew all that weighed so heavily on her. Time stood still as she soaked in His comfort, but her peace would be unattainable until the twins' return.

"There you are," Ross said from behind her.

She jumped up then whirled to face him. "Why did you stay gone so long?"

"The kids were having a good time and Nanny and Papaw loved having them. We kind of lost track of time."

"I thought you weren't coming back." Her voice broke.

"I can't believe after all this time, after all of my assurances and meeting my parents, you still don't trust me." Ross's shoulders slumped and he closed his eyes.

"You should have called me."

"Maybe." A tic developed in his jaw. "But I shouldn't have to. I said we'd be back and I meant it."

"People say things they don't mean all the time."

"I don't." He jerked his Stetson off, ran his fingers through his hair, then clamped it back in place. "You know what? I'm done. I'm done trying to win your trust, much less your heart. I'll go clear out my apartment and stay with my folks in Bandera tonight. Tomorrow, I'll come say bye to the twins and that's the last you'll see of me. And in the future, when we come to visit them, I'll do my best to avoid you." He stalked away toward the house.

Stacia leaned on her knees and the let the tears flow. The only thing wrong with him leaving was that her heart had betrayed her, despite her best efforts. And if by some chance she could trust him, it still could never work out between them. He wanted kids and she could never give him that.

The only good part of the equation was that he hadn't said anything about taking the kids with them to Houston. She needed to focus on that. Mason and Madison weren't going anywhere.

She mopped her face, tried to pull herself together and followed the path home.

Chapter Thirteen

A few minutes later, as she neared the house, Ross's mom waved from the porch.

"Stacia." Karen met her. "Are you all right?"

"Allergies."

"Oh, I was hoping you'd go for a walk with me so I won't get lost, even though you just went on one. But maybe you need to get inside away from all the irritants."

"I'm fine. Let's go."

Karen linked arms with her. "I want to thank you for making this transition so easy for everyone. For allowing us to spend the day with Mason and Madison. My folks were thrilled to meet them."

"You're welcome." Though it had ripped her heart in two.

"Madison is so grown-up, it's amazing. And Mason is so full of—life."

"Is that what it is?" Stacia chuckled. "He's so much like my sister. A great kid, but don't leave him to his own devices cause when he gets bored, look out."

"Ron was the same way." Sadness cloaked Karen's tone. "And Ross was so easy. Like a little grown-up. Just like

Madison, and I suspect you were the same. They're complete treasures."

"They are." Guilt pierced her heart. The Lyleses had missed so many years of Mason's and Madison's lives. "You should have been in their lives from the beginning. I'm sorry I never tried to find out if they had other family members. Ron said he didn't have any family and I wanted to believe him."

"I understand, dear." Karen gave her a soothing pat on the arm. "You love them and you were afraid we'd try to take them away from you. You still are."

"A little."

"You can relax. Madison and Mason are clearly happy, loved and well-cared for here with you. You and Maverick love them to the marrow of your souls. If they didn't have a good home life or if they didn't have y'all, it would be a different story. But as it is..." Karen sighed. "I've raised my children and apparently with a fifty-fifty rate of success. I'm completely content being a grandparent now and leaving the raising to you."

"Thank you." It was all Stacia could squeak out.

"Ron hasn't been home to see us in years because we always hounded him about seeking treatment for alcoholism. He probably felt he was telling the truth about not having family." She gazed off into the treetops. "He only came home this time because he needed a caretaker after his wreck. And after the trip here, he left again. I just hope he stays in the treatment center."

"I'm sorry. All of that had to be rough on you."

"I pray for him and hold on to Proverbs 22:6, 'Train up a child in the way he should go: and when he is old, he will not depart from it.' I go to sleep at night repeating it silently. It gives me peace, helps me remember that Sam and I have done all we can. It's up to God now. We were hoping the wreck would be a wake-up call."

"It still can be. He did go to a treatment center." It was strange talking about Ron this way since she'd feared him for so long.

"I pray so. But I know exactly how it feels to lose a child. I wouldn't wish it on anyone and I certainly wouldn't cause it by suing you for custody. Just keep taking care of them, put up with our visits and everything will be fine."

"I can do that." Except that she dreaded occasionally bumping into Ross for years to come.

"I hope you won't lose Ross."

"What?"

"He's in love with you, Stacia."

"You're mistaken."

"No. A mother knows these things. He doesn't have ulterior motives, you know. He only wants to be an uncle to the twins with frequent visits. The look I've seen in his eye, is all about you."

Flustered, Stacia's skin heated. Could Karen be right? Even if she was, there was still her inability to have children to contend with. No, she and Ross could never work. No matter how badly she wanted it.

"I'm sorry to get so personal, dear. I just wanted to share a little insight. But on another note, last night Sam and I toyed with the idea of moving to San Antonio."

"Really? That's only an hour away."

"We've discussed moving the store for years. San Antonio is only forty-five minutes from Sam's folks in Hondo and we're so very tired of hurricanes. With the twins in Medina, the scales have tilted in favor of the move."

"That would be wonderful." Since they'd finished their deep discussion and she was eager to see the kids, Stacia looped their walk back toward the house.

"Are you certain? We don't want to crowd you."

"The kids would love having you so close and visiting back and forth would be so much easier."

"Aunt Stacia." Madison jogged out to meet them.

But Mason passed her up and made it first. "We had so much fun with Nanny and Papaw."

"I'm so glad." Stacia really was glad and it almost made her teary to think about all of the new family members who could love the twins now. Or maybe relief, since it was finally beginning to sink in that she could keep her niece and nephew.

"That's what my folks have always been called by the grands. Sam decided on Paw since they already call Maverick Grandpa. And I'm Nana."

"We went from having one grandpa to four new grandparents in two days." Madison skipped beside them.

"I bet not many kids do that." Stacia's enthusiasm was finally unforced.

"We grocery shopped on the way home, so you get to relax tonight. I'm cooking." Karen let go of Stacia's arm and hugged her. "I better get started."

"You don't have to do that."

"No. But I want to. It's the least we can do since we showed up and rocked your world out of the blue." Karen hurried toward the house.

"Nanny has the coolest store," Mason piped up. "Kind of like ours, but different."

"I've been there. It is cool."

"You know Nanny?" Madison frowned.

"I do. I've shopped in her store. But I didn't know she was y'alls nanny until recently."

"Uncle Ross talked about you a lot." Mason rolled his eyes.

Stacia's breath stilled. "He did?"

"I think he's sweet on you." Madison giggled. "He said he missed you because he's used to spending the day with you in the store."

Her heart fluttered at that. "I think he was probably just being nice."

"I don't think so." Madison shook her head. "Wouldn't it be cool if you and Uncle Ross got married?"

"Yuck." Mason gagged. "Mushy stuff."

"Don't worry." She tousled his hair as they climbed the porch steps. "There won't be any mushy stuff between me and your uncle."

"I'm gonna go help Nana with supper." Madison darted inside.

"I'll go see what the menfolk are doing." Mason sounded so grown-up as he followed.

Stacia's knees were suddenly weak and she sank to the porch swing. Had she misjudged Ross? He knew she couldn't have kids, yet he'd claimed to have feelings for her. But he'd told Madison he hoped to marry and have kids someday.

Even if the feelings he'd professed for her were real, she could never take the chance of getting pregnant. She knew what it was like to lose a mother. And a sister. She could never risk leaving behind motherless children.

Could his feelings really be as genuine as hers? Why would he be willing to give up the possibility of biological children for a future with her?

She hurried inside, bolted up the stairs for her room.

But Daddy met her in the hallway. He held an envelope toward her. "You need to read this."

Foreboding crept a chill down her spine. "What is it?"

"A letter. From Aunt Eleanor. I should have given it to you back when I first got it."

"When was that?" Her voice quivered.

"After Callista died. She sent me one too. Took me about a year to read it. I read yours as well, to help me decide if you needed to. They're both quite enlightening, but I knew it would stir bad memories and I was afraid it might bring back the nightmares you used to have. So I held on to it."

"Until now?" She swallowed hard.

"I think it might help you. To move on."

Aunt Eleanor's actions had colored her life, her perception of other people. Her perception of Ross. Her perception of God. Daddy was right. She was stuck.

Her hand shook as she took it from him.

"Want me to stick around while you read it?"

"No." She darted for her room, shut the door. On wobbly legs, she leaned against it, sank to the floor. The envelope sliced into her trembling finger as she fished the letter out and unfolded it.

Dear Stacia,

You're an adult now and I hope you'll accept my heartfelt apology.

If only I hadn't made such a mess of things. Instead of having a relationship with my nieces, I ended up hiding behind a tree at Callista's funeral. I loved her.

And you.

Please keep reading as I try to explain. Right after your mom died and they found the hereditary heart condition, I was mourning my sister and worried about my own health since all of the women in our family died young, but no one ever figured out why. Until your mom.

So I went to see my doctor and learned I have the defect. He told me not to have children. I was distraught, so of course I shared the news with my fiancé.

Since he wanted kids, it was a deal breaker for him.

For the first time, Stacia felt empathy for her aunt. Mourning over her sister, and then the man she planned to spend the rest of her life with dumped her. What a jerk. Even though Stacia hadn't been in love with Adrian, and he hadn't known about her medical condition, him rejecting the twins had hurt. She kept reading.

I knew your father needed help with you girls and I wanted to get away from my situation, so I came to live with y'all. It was all innocent to begin with. But as time passed, I got it in my head that things would be easier on your dad if I took you girls off his hands. And that if I had two girls to raise, Thad would come back to me and marry me.

It all made so much more sense now. Still twisted, but the story helped her understand her aunt's state of mind back then.

I'm not a bad person. I'm really not. But I've been punished more than any prison term could have done. I could have adopted children, gotten on with my life. Instead I wasted my heart on a man who was unworthy of me—I never married and spent most of my life alone. If only I'd realized Thad was a clod sooner, I could have had a relationship with my nieces and my great-niece and -nephew.

Of course I saw them at the funeral. I assume they're Callista's and was hoping I might come see y'all one day. Just promise me, you'll pray about forgiving me. About restoring our relationship. I really do love you, Stacia. And I'm truly sorry. Your loving,

Aunt Eleanor

Stacia pressed the letter against her heart. It brought back all the memories she'd tried to bury. The terror of never seeing her father again. Of Calli sobbing on her shoulder, while Stacia's eyes stung with trying to be strong for her little sister. The nightmares that had plagued her since. For years it had been her and Calli torn away from their home or lost and unable to find their way back. Once the twins had been born, the nightmares had featured them instead.

"Dear Lord," she whispered. "I'm tired of being scared. Tired of being suspicious of everyone. Tired of not trusting anyone. Tired of not fully trusting You. I'm sorry for trying to keep everyone safe without You. For being so stubborn. I don't want to be in control anymore."

Peace threaded through her. Complete peace she hadn't had since her mom's death.

A knock on her door vibrated against her back.

She swiped her face, folded the letter, put it back in the envelope and stood. "Come in."

Daddy stuck his head in. "You okay?"

"Not really." She shook her head, sank to the edge of her bed.

"You read it?" He stepped in, closed the door behind him, plopped on the bed beside her and gave her a hug. "Oh sweetheart."

"It actually helped."

"I hoped it would."

"Ross told me he has feelings for me and I accused him of pretending, so he could get custody of the twins."

"Just like Aunt Eleanor." Daddy sighed. "You have to apologize. Have you told him about your aunt?"

"Not really."

"Tell him, sweetheart. He'll understand."

"It's too late. And even if it wasn't, I can't have kids."

"Does Ross know that?"

"Yes."

"And he still has feelings for you, so he must be okay with that."

"Maybe. But even if he is, is it fair for me to sentence him to a life of never having a biological child?"

"If we'd known about your mom's health, I wouldn't have considered it a sentence. I loved her. You have to talk to him."

Daddy was right, she needed to at least apologize. Maybe nothing could ever happen between her and Ross, but she still owed him an apology.

Ross had barely slept last night. The rental cabin was nice with a comfortable bed. But his mind had been stuck on Stacia. His heart hurt and he couldn't wait to get back to Houston, to get on with his life without her. Since he'd had the argument with Stacia and his parents knew he was hurting, they'd agreed not to stay for church.

He pulled into the familiar drive for the last time with a heavy heart. Maverick waved from the porch swing as Ross got out of his truck. His parents turned in behind him.

As Texan hospitality would have it, Maverick had insisted on cooking them breakfast before they headed out. Ross had considered staying at the cabin, but he wanted to see the twins before he left. And he didn't want to insult Maverick's gesture.

One more tense meal of trying to ignore Stacia and he'd be free.

"Can we talk, privately?" Maverick met him with a handshake.

"Sure."

"Sam, Karen, so glad you could make it." Maverick greeted his folks. "I'm afraid we're a bit behind here. Our mutual grandkids aren't even up yet and Stacia's in the workshop, finishing up a baby gift for her friend."

"You don't have to bother with breakfast," Mom said. "We can visit with the twins a bit and then eat on the road."

"Nonsense. We'll get it together. Y'all can go on in and wake the kiddos if you want."

"We'll definitely take you up on that." Dad rubbed his palms together the way he did when things went his way.

"I'll get breakfast going in a jiffy." Maverick waited until Mom and Dad went inside, then turned to Ross. "Have a seat."

Ross settled on the porch swing and Maverick plopped down on the opposite end.

"I can't let you leave without explaining a few things."

"Okay."

"After Emilia, my wife, died, Callista had a really rough time with it. Stacia was always the strong, stoic one. Not so much for my youngest. So Eleanor, Emilia's younger sister, came to stay with us for a while. I was in over my head with two girls and grieving my wife, so I welcomed her help. But after a while, things got weird."

"How so?"

"It seemed like she was trying to take Emilia's place. In the house, in the girls' hearts and in mine. She became less sisterly and set her sights on me. I told her I thought the world of her, but not in that way. She was embarrassed and planned to go back home."

Maverick stared off in the distance, lost in memories. "But just as she was supposed to leave, I got a bad case of bronchitis, so I asked her to stay and take care of the girls until I was up to it. She drove us to the doctor and then the pharmacy. I went in to get my medication and when I came out, they were gone."

"She took them?" Stacia's hang-up suddenly made sense.

"Yes. At first, I thought maybe she'd gone to get the girls ice cream or something. I didn't feel well, so a friend drove me home and I left a message on Eleanor's cell phone that I'd gone home. When she didn't call back, I started getting worried. That's when I listened to the answering machine." Maverick closed his eyes. "I'll never forget the words. 'Maverick, I just can't leave the girls behind. Don't worry, I'll take care of them as if they were my own. I'm sorry.'"

"Did you call the police?"

"No. I knew if my Emilia was alive, she wouldn't want her sister going to prison. I'd gotten the girls a cell phone and I had a computer guru friend." Maverick seemed to age as he told the story. Shoulders slumped, more lines on his face.

"I called him and he was able to track them. They were headed toward Dallas. I have no idea where she planned to go. I called her and left a message that I'd put a tracking device on her car and that if she didn't immediately turn around and bring the girls home, I'd call the police."

"So she did, right?"

"At first, we watched her red dot on my friend's laptop stop. As if she was weighing her options. I tell you, in that moment, I was petrified I'd made the wrong call. That she'd decide if she couldn't have the girls, no one would." Maverick's voice cracked. "It was the most terrifying moment of my life. But then she turned around. And I knew my girls were coming home."

With how Ross felt about the twins in such a short time of knowing them, he couldn't imagine how Maverick must have felt. Or Stacia and Callista for that matter. They'd probably loved their aunt and definitely trusted her.

"They were home within two hours. Physically fine, but mentally traumatized. I told Eleanor to never come near us again or I'd have her arrested."

Such behavior from someone you loved and trusted would do a number on your ability to love and trust in the future. No wonder Stacia had issues.

"But it still wasn't over. Eleanor served me with papers, suing me for custody."

"You can't be serious?" Tension built in Ross's chest.

"Dead serious. I had no proof she'd kidnapped the girls since I never called the police. It was my word against hers."

"What about your friend or the girls?"

"My friend was considered an unreliable witness since he was my friend. And the girls were having nightmares. I couldn't let them be called to the stand. In the end, I won. There was no proof that I was negligent like Eleanor claimed."

"So what happened to her?"

"She went away and we never heard from her again. Until Calli died. She sent two letters, one for me and one for Stacia. It took me a year to open them." Maverick gave the rundown on everything Eleanor had said. "My letter confirmed my suspicions, her trying to romance me was all a ruse. She just wanted the girls."

"Has Stacia read hers?"

"After I read them, I was afraid they'd give her nightmares again, so I tucked them away. Until last night. I gave her the letter, hoping it might help her put everything behind her."

"How is she?"

"She's okay. I think it cleared some things up for her. Understanding why Eleanor acted the way she did helped her come to terms with her aunt. And it helped her confront her own trust issues." Maverick clapped him on the shoulder. "That your first question concerns my daughter's welfare proves my theory. You're in love with her."

"Yes, sir."

"I think she's got it bad for you too, my boy. And if you want to pursue something with her, you should go talk to her. I think she's ready to hear you out. To trust."

"Thank you, sir. If she'll have me, I'll do my best to never hurt her."

"I'm aware of that, my boy. Now go on, while I rustle up some vittles."

Ross stepped off the porch, trying to play it cool. But he couldn't pull it off. He loped for the workshop.

The doors were open. Inside, Stacia stood at the worktable with her back to him, securing deer antlers on a slab of wood above the name *Rand* spelled out in tin letters. He stood watching as love and understanding welled up inside him with a strong desire to provide comfort for the wounds her aunt had inflicted.

She turned, got a glimpse of him. "Is breakfast ready?"

"No."

"Then why are you here? You don't work here anymore."

He ambled over to her, drew her into his arms.

"What are you doing?" She was all stiff.

"I'm hugging you. This is called a hug."

"Why? Oh, is this goodbye?" She relaxed a bit, raised her hands to his shoulders, but didn't really hug him back.

"No. I'm hugging you because I love you."

"But I didn't believe you. And accused you of trying to take the twins from me. I thought you were mad and giving up on me."

"Your dad told me about your aunt. About the letter you read last night. Why didn't you tell me? I would have understood your distrust, your phobia, if you'd just told me what she did."

Her arms finally came around his neck. "It's still hard to talk about." Her voice broke as she went all soft, leaning into him, seeking comfort he was more than willing to provide.

"I'm so sorry you had to go through all that. I can't imagine."

"The worst part was Calli whimpering on my shoulder, wanting to go home. And me promising her we'd see Daddy again, when I didn't know if we would or not." Her words ended on a sob.

"It's okay now." Ross held her, stroking her hair. "I'd take away all your pain and the memories, if I could."

"I'm sorry for not trusting you. For accusing you of trying to steal the twins."

"If I'd been through what you have, I probably would've thought the same thing. It's okay."

Eventually, the tears stopped and she stilled. "How can I forgive her? I mean, the Bible says we're supposed to forgive. And if Jesus can forgive the people who crucified Him, I should forgive Eleanor."

"He also knows we're human. Just pray about it."

She nodded against him, then pulled away. Tear streaks traced down her cheeks, leaving a trail through her makeup, revealing the freckles he loved. And none of it took away from her beauty.

"Look, I know you're dealing with some things. And there's no rush, but I love you, Stacia. I'd like to come on the weekends to see you. And when you're ready, I'd like to be part of your life. Maybe take you on a date."

But she was shaking her head before he even finished. Obviously still unable to trust that his feelings were real.

"The way I see it, since my family is probably moving to San Antonio and you're being so accommodating in letting them see the twins, me romancing you won't help anything. Except my happiness. How about dinner tomorrow night?"

"Not a good idea."

He swallowed hard. "You don't have feelings for me?"

"I didn't say that."

"Then what?"

"I can't have kids, Ross. I won't take the chance of leaving motherless children behind. I've been there."

"Aren't you getting a bit ahead of things?" He chuckled, trying to lighten her mood. "I'm just talking about dinner."

Her cheeks tinged pink and she pulled away, turned her back on him. "But dinner—and feelings—can lead to marriage, and you want kids, so how can there be a future for us? I mean, if I only risk one pregnancy and I don't have twins, maybe I could survive, but I can't chance it. I won't be responsible for leaving motherless—"

"Stop." He gently gripped her shoulders, turned her to face him, and pressed a finger against her lips. "I'd never ask you to do that. Never. You're too important to me. But it sounds like you do have feelings for me?" He held his breath.

Her almost imperceptible nod sent his heart into overdrive.

"I do want kids," he admitted, weighing his words carefully. "I love the twins. And they're not mine. If it works out between us—and I'm praying it does—there are a lot of children in the world looking for good homes. I'm pretty sure we could provide one filled with love."

"Adoption? You'd be okay with that?"

"More than okay."

She swiped her eyes. "I'm a mess."

"You're beautiful." He cupped her face in his hands. "So how about that dinner?"

Tears rimmed her lashes as she met his gaze. "I'd like that."

He lowered his lips to hers.

"Wait."

"Wait?"

"I need to wash my face before you kiss me."

"I've wanted to kiss you for weeks and I'm not waiting a second longer."

Her breath caught as their lips met.

Soft and yielding. Sweet and addictive. Trusting. The last woman he'd ever kiss.

Epilogue

"I do." Stacia smiled up at Ross.

"By the power vested in me, I pronounce you husband and wife. You may kiss your bride."

"You're my wife now. Forever," Ross whispered as he drew her into his arms. Gentle as if she were a rare treasure.

Her breath stilled as her hands slid up his shoulders. His toe-curling kiss made her heart giddy. Every time. Even after a year of dating.

"Ladies and gentlemen, I present Mr. and Mrs. Ross Lyles."

The crowd applauded as the piano started up. Mason and Madison walked the aisle toward the back of the church, followed by Larae and Lexie, then Ross's best friend from high school and Sam.

Ross escorted her to the fellowship hall to form a line so guests could congratulate them.

"I don't know about you," he whispered close to her ear, sending a shiver over her, "but I'd like to get out of the penguin suit and split."

"Stop. Everybody here loves us and wants to share in our happiness."

"I know. And I appreciate them. But couldn't we have done all this before the ceremony?"

Denny and Stella made it to them first.

"Child, I sure wish your mama could see you." Stella adjusted the train of Mom's dress.

"Me too." Stacia's gaze went misty.

"You're the spitting image of her." Stella winked.

"Thanks. And thank you for being a wonderful stand-in mom all these years."

"My pleasure." Stella hugged her.

"That goes for me too." Lexie joined in their hug and dragged Larae in too. "And thank you, Larae, for sharing your mom with us."

Larae fanned her face with one hand. "Y'all stop. We're all gonna be blubbering and have to repair our makeup before pictures."

"Pictures." Ross groaned.

"Might as well settle in." Clint, Lexie's newlywed husband, grinned. "This will be the longest day of your life."

It had been fun to see the friendship develop between Ross and her two best friends' husbands over the last year.

"I just want to ride off into the sunset with my bride." He drew her against his side, then stiffened. "Ron, what are you doing here?"

Stacia's gaze jerked to her husband, then to his brother, standing in front of them, then to the twins. They were oblivious, putting up with hugs from other well-wishers.

"I came to give you a wedding gift," Ron said.

With his career in high gear, Ron had remained clean and sober since his accident. Minus his goth makeup, blue hair, and with him looking healthy, no one would recognize him.

"This should be enough to put a down payment on a house." He held up a check.

Stacia's eyes widened at all the zeroes. "I'm not sure we'd feel right about accepting it."

"Please, let me do this for my big brother," Ron whispered. "I owe you a lot more than that. And I figure you can use some of it for legal fees to formally adopt the twins."

Stacia gasped as tears threatened. "That's the best gift you could ever give me."

"They deserve a real family. And a house." Ron folded the check in half and tucked it in Ross's tux pocket, then hugged him.

"You saw Mom and Dad?"

"Yes. And if it's okay with y'all, I might start coming around more often. Maybe for Christmas."

"That sounds wonderful." Ross caught her gaze. "As long as you're okay with it?"

"Of course."

"What do we tell those two?" Ron nodded toward Mason and Madison.

"We'll figure something out." Stacia hugged him. "Thank you, Ron."

"Thank you for taking such good care of them." It was there, the glint in his eyes. He knew he was missing out. But it didn't frighten her anymore. "I'm honored to get to."

"See y'all soon." Ron turned toward the exit.

"Did that really just happen? The biggest fear in my life just turned out to be harmless."

"God fixed everything." He pulled her into his arms. "Can we get out of here yet?"

"That would be rude."

He kissed her into silence.

"Ewww!" Mason cringed.

"Break it up, you two." Madison giggled.

"Y'all better get used to it." Ross chuckled. "I plan to kiss my wife a lot."

"You better." Her heart was full. The twins were hers. And so was their uncle. Their happily-ever-after was better than anything she'd ever dreamed of.

* * * * *

Dear Reader,

Inspired by *Flea Market Flip* and *Salvage Dawgs*, my husband and I rented a booth. We enjoyed repurposing furniture and crafting junk decor. But the time and labor involved equaled dismal sales and only the owner turned a profit. We dream of owning a flea market someday and watching our vendors work while we run the register and a side booth.

I had a blast fashioning a *Salvage Dawgs* type store for Stacia Keyes. Like me, Stacia is a sensible rule follower, juggling responsibilities. Unlike me, she's raising her twin niece and nephew. She considers herself damaged and focuses solely on keeping her loved ones safe.

Like Stacia, Ross Lyles is the older, wiser sibling, but his connection to the twins terrifies her. He's determined to be an uncle and make up for his brother's abandonment. With Stacia questioning his every move, he's intent on a peaceful solution and what's best for the twins.

Finally, they realize they're not in control, God is. As their fears melt away, He paves the way for their happily-ever-after.

This is the final book in my Hill Country Cowboys series. I'll miss these characters and the ranches based on family property in my second home, Medina, Texas. I hope y'all loved vicariously living there.

Shannon

COMING NEXT MONTH FROM
Love Inspired

Available March 30, 2021

THE BABY NEXT DOOR
Indiana Amish Brides • by Vannetta Chapman

When Grace Troyer and her baby girl move back home, the Amish bachelor next door can't resist the little family. But Adrian Schrock's plan to nudge Grace out of her shell by asking her to cook for *Englischers* on his farm tour might just expose secrets Grace hopes to keep buried...

THE AMISH TEACHER'S WISH
by Tracey J. Lyons

With the school damaged during a storm, teacher Sadie Fischer needs Levi Byler's help repairing it. As they work together, Levi's determined he *won't* become a part of her search for a husband. But Sadie might be the perfect woman to mend his heart...and convince him forever isn't just for fairy tales.

REBUILDING HER LIFE
Kendrick Creek • by Ruth Logan Herne

Home to help rebuild her mother's clinic after a forest fire, Jess Bristol never expects Shane Stone—the man she once wrongfully sent to jail—to arrive with the same purpose. But as sparks fly between them and she falls for the children in his care, can their troubled past lead to a happy future?

A TRUE COWBOY
Double R Legacy • by Danica Favorite

The last thing William Bennett ever thought he'd do was plan a benefit rodeo, but it's the perfect way to move on after his ex-fiancée's betrayal. But his partner on the project, single and pregnant Grace Duncan, is scaling the walls around his heart...with a secret that could destroy their budding love.

HER SECRET HOPE
by Lorraine Beatty

With her life and career in tatters, journalist Melody Williams takes a job working on a book about the history of a small town—and discovers her boss is the father of the child she gave up. Clay Reynolds secretly adopted their little boy, but can he trust Melody with the truth...and their son?

THEIR FAMILY ARRANGEMENT
by Angel Moore

After they lose their best friends in a tragic accident, former high school sweethearts Kevin Lane and Sophie Owens will do anything to keep the two orphaned children left in their custody. So when a judge insists on a couple to parent the children, a temporary engagement is the only solution...

LOOK FOR THESE AND OTHER LOVE INSPIRED BOOKS WHEREVER BOOKS ARE SOLD, INCLUDING MOST BOOKSTORES, SUPERMARKETS, DISCOUNT STORES AND DRUGSTORES.

LICNM0321

When a young Amish woman returns home with a baby in tow, will sparks fly with her handsome—and unusual—neighbor?

Read on for a sneak preview of
The Baby Next Door
by Vannetta Chapman.

Grace found Nicole had pulled herself up to the front door and was high-fiving none other than Adrian Schrock. He'd squatted down to her level. Nicole was having a fine old time.

Grace picked up her *doschder* and pushed open the door, causing Adrian to jump up, then step back toward the porch steps. It was, indeed, a fine spring day. The sun shone brightly across the Indiana fields. Flowers colored yellow, red, lavender and orange had begun popping through the soil that surrounded the porch. Birds were even chirping merrily.

Somehow, all those things did little to elevate Grace's mood. Neither did the sight of her neighbor.

Adrian resettled his straw hat on his head and smiled. *"Gudemariye."*

"Your llama has escaped again."

"Kendrick? *Ya.* I've come to fetch him. He seems to like your place more than mine."

"I don't want that animal over here, Adrian. He spits. And your peacock was here at daybreak, crying like a child."

LIEXP0321

Adrian laughed. "When you moved back home, I guess you didn't expect to live next to a Plain & Simple Exotic Animal Farm."

Adrian wiggled his eyebrows at Nicole when he seemed to realize that Grace wasn't amused.

"I think of your place as Adrian's Zoo."

"Not a bad name, but it doesn't highlight our Amish heritage enough."

"The point is that I feel like we're living next door to a menagerie of animals."

"Up, Aden. Up."

Adrian scooped Nicole from Grace's hold, held her high above his head, then nuzzled her neck. Adrian was comfortable with everyone and everything.

"Do you think she'll ever learn to say my name right?"

"Possibly. Can you please catch Kendrick and take him back to your place?"

"Of course. That's why I came over. I guess I must have left the gate open again." He kissed Nicole's cheek, then popped her back into Grace's arms. "You should bring her over to see the turtles."

As he walked away, Grace wondered for the hundredth time why he wasn't married. It was true that he'd picked a strange profession. What other Amish man raised exotic animals? No, Adrian wouldn't be considered excellent marrying material by most young Amish women.

Don't miss
The Baby Next Door *by Vannetta Chapman,*
available April 2021 wherever
Love Inspired books and ebooks are sold.

LoveInspired.com

LIEXP0321